Black Wings

Veliz Books' titles are available to the trade through our website and our primary distributor, Small Press Distribution (800) 869.7553. For personal orders, catalogs, or other information, write to info@velizbooks.com.

For further information write Veliz Books:
P.O. Box 920243, El Paso, TX 79902
velizbooks.com

ISBN 9781949776003

Black Wings

SEHBA SARWAR

velizbooks.com

To my father the late Dr. Mohammad Sarwar for the social consciousness that he wove into our family fabric, and to my mother Zakia Sarwar for her strength.

Yasmeen wakes up, stretches her arms over her head, but does not need to open her eyes to know that at four in the morning, Yasir sleepwalked into her room. Her twin is asleep, bunched up against the wall with his legs folded close to his chest. His head drops low and his breath stirs his curly hair. A notebook and pen lie on the floor beside his slippers. In Hawagali, Yasir usually sleeps in the attic, but the twins are accustomed to waking up in each other's rooms, sometimes on chairs, sometimes on the floor, and often in the same bed.

Yasir's body jerks as his eyes flash open. "It was about us flying..."

"... to Hawagali." She finishes his sentence. That is what they do.

He sits up and circles his neck. "So how did it end?"

They know how their dreams work. Sometimes he sees the beginning, she the end—and sometimes vice versa—but their dreams are incomplete if they don't share them with each other. Fully awake, Yasmeen grabs the camera that her aunt gave her, and the twins race through the verandah to the back of their summer house. The sunshine is warm, and they want to spend every moment outside. Yasir stops by the kitchen's screen-door and slips three cigarettes wrapped in newspaper under the water pot for Riaz, the cook, to retrieve when he takes a break. Yasir, always there to help anyone who needs it, supplies Riaz with the Dunhills he loves but cannot afford. Yasmeen taps her brother's head as she races past him. In return, he grimaces at her and wags his thumbs in his ears.

Yasmeen and Yasir clamber up the side wooden stairs to the open rooftop so they can reach their secret hangout—the forbidden section of their Hawagali mountain home—on the rooftop chajja, the ledge without a wall. Yasir, taller than his sister, heaves her over the wall so she can reach the other side, then he scrambles over to join her. The seventeen-year-olds lie on the warm aluminum, staring past fir tree-tops at the distant snow-clad Himalayan peaks.

"The beginning was you, me, and Amman," Yasir says. "We're leaving Karachi and Abu and... we're flying to Hawagali. We wear black wings, you know, like kaneez robes, but we look like bats or crows—"

"—and then," she interrupts, "we're on the ground in front of a cave. The hollow cave opens onto a beach, but we can see the mountains in the background. We can't decide what we want to do, and we start shouting at each other. You break away from us and vanish in the cave—it's like Ali Baba's cave. I separate from Amman and fly up toward the mountaintop."

"And Amman?" Yasir's eyes are closed.

She shakes her head. "I don't know. I lost it."

Yasir sits up. "Wait. I know. Amman doesn't move. She remains beneath the fir trees and palm trees all mixed together. Trees sway around her. I emerge from the cave and join her. We wait for you but you don't return. We just see you flying and laughing. We miss you but we're happy that you're having fun."

They sigh. "Yes, that's it."

Sitting up, Yasmeen pulls out her new camera from its case. Yasir hides his face between his knees and wraps his elbows around his body. When he looks up, his twin starts clicking.

After Yasir is gone, when Yasmeen gets the roll developed at Karachi's Car Studio, she finds that the black and white shots are out of focus, except one, which is only slightly blurry. In the photo, Yasir's laugh makes his uneven teeth glisten. His eyes are crinkled and strands of his hair cast pencil shadows on his high forehead. Barefoot, with his toes flexed, the bottom of Yasir's soles are caked with dirt. Encased in his long fingers is a cigarette that he holds close to his mouth; he is not puffing because he cannot stop laughing at his twin who tries to adjust her new gadget, maneuver the lens, adjust the light, and click, all at the right time. He reaches his toe forward and tickles her foot, distracting Yasmeen even more. Yasir's laughter is a gurgle that remains locked in Yasmeen's mind, long after Yasir is no more.

When Yasmeen studies the photo, she notices a black speck floating over Yasir's head. The mark appears to be an ink smudge, but when she studies it under a microscope she thinks the streak might be a crow. She also knows that the dot could be something else.

The photograph is framed in every relative's house all over Pakistan, and is also in Yasmeen's Houston studio. For her, the black and white print is a reminder of how the only time she uses her camera is to capture the final image of her seventeen-year-old twin.

BOOK ONE

one

YASMEEN

I hesitated behind the wheel, hoping to sight Amman exiting the terminal doors that sprang open, but the woman who walked toward my car clutched an empty birdcage and was not my mother.

A blue-uniformed policeman strode toward me, signaling me to move my car: "Take it round, ma'am. Go! Go! Now!"

I inched forward behind a Lexus SUV, which had picked up a group of tanned teenagers. They had probably returned from a trip to the Bahamas, I muttered to myself. According to experts, air travel had declined since September, and those who were willing to fly had found cheap airline deals this winter.

As I pulled away from the curb to circle one more time around Houston's Mickey Leland International Terminal, I looked through my rearview mirror and caught sight of passengers wearing shalwar kurtas—their faces ravaged from a tough entry into the US—trickling out. I slammed my brakes; Amman's flight had arrived. But I was too late, the policeman was back at my window. "Move, ma'am!"

I gave up and surrendered to drive yet another circle. The hourly parking garage had been closed, and gone were the days when one could park close to the terminal and saunter up to a gate to welcome family.

I completed my fifth round and I pulled up at the terminal to hear a Pakistani man scolding his wife in Urdu, telling her to switch to

English and to strive—somehow—to blend in amidst men and women outlined by jeans, sweatshirts, and baseball caps. I had not spoken Urdu for a long time, but my ears caught the language, and to my surprise, enjoyed the lilt that I had not heard or spoken for years.

My eyes roved through bodies that exited the terminal. Next to stationary red and yellow luggage trolleys, I spotted her, a tall woman in a blue sari. Amman—chatting with a Pakistani man who wore a jacket too small for him around the shoulders.

She had not noticed me, yet. Holding back for a moment, I studied her through my tinted window. She was heavier than when I had seen her ten years ago, but for her late fifties, with her dyed black hair pulled in a bun at the base of her neck, she looked well. Her smooth face, dark as a walnut, and her deep voice sent me back to a younger Amman laughing with her head tossed back at our Hawagali mountain home, and walking beside Yasir and me on low-backed horses as we inhaled the fragrance of crushed pine, wood smoke, and clove-spiced tea.

In the hazy Houston afternoon light, Amman's eyes met mine. Leaving her luggage cart with her friend, she strode towards my car, a steamship riding a turbulent ocean. I fumbled with my door handle but of course the door was locked—where did I get this compulsion to lock everything all the time? The door clicked open, and I jumped onto the parking divider. Amman's smile weakened my knees. She reached me and pulled me close to her chest.

"Had a safe flight?" I felt out of breath, as if I had been running for a day without a break.

She nodded, smiling.

"No problem with immigration?" I forced myself to breathe.

Her eyes did not leave mine as she shook her head.

"You have your luggage?"

She opened her mouth, her Urdu taking me by surprise.

"Yes. The children?"

"At school."

"And you, Baita, how are you?"

Baita. Genderless word for child. Amman had called me Baita in that tone since I was a toddler. Not Baiti—daughter. I did not mind now, just as I had not minded then. I watched her straight back swim away from me as she collected her luggage cart. I loaded her suitcases into the trunk, conscious of her quietness—which was different from

14

the Amman in Karachi that I remembered: Amman, getting ready for a party, applying lipstick and laughing into her reflection, letting me choose her sari for the evening, teaching me how to set the table, where to place the knives and forks, how to greet visitors, and what to offer them.

In the car, she reclined, her eyes half-closed. I marveled at how she was able to dismiss the airport chaos. I had been away from Karachi for so long that I had forgotten that most airports around the world allowed only passengers into terminals. I had never thought that the same would happen in the US.

"Airport security's insane," I said, making conversation. "Did you have any problems?"

Amman shook her head. "No, no, but the man I was speaking to had to open out his whole suitcase. The immigration lady asked him many questions. We were thinking he'd be sent back. Finally, they let him go. In London, so many people were searched. I don't know what the world's come to."

"No problems getting a visa?"

"I have connections, you know, in the Consulate. Of course, I had to fly to Islamabad to get the visa. But your Manzoor Mamoon— you remember him? He was refused even though his son has cancer. But that's what they're doing. Making it impossible for our men to travel. And if men wear beards, they should just forget about flying to America."

"Awful."

"And you, are you having problems here?"

"Not too much." Not ready to take the conversation into a direction that I had not yet processed, I didn't want to bring up the incident at Saira's school. I had been living in the States for almost two decades, and I always felt as if I could slip in and out of spaces without being marked as a "foreigner," a Pakistani, or a Muslim. I wore western clothes, and most times people assumed that I was from Mexico or another Latin American country. But something was changing—either in me or around me—and I no longer felt as inconspicuous as before.

Amman's eyes scanned my linen skirt and my black heels, rested for a second on the white strip around my ring finger where my marriage band had been, before her gaze flickered past me. I tightened my grip on the wheel. In the invitation that I had sent her a month earlier, I mentioned that Jim and I had ended our marriage. Glad that she had not approached the subject, I fixed my eyes on Beltway Eight, the circular freeway outside Houston's center. Amman gazed out of the window, and I wondered what she thought of the adult sex billboards that lined the freeway every thirty yards. She could not be shocked—Karachi had its sights with strewn litter, no pavements, broken roads, and men pissing against already stained walls.

We approached the city center, and a cluster of buildings stretched into the sky like metallic blue pencils. "Downtown Houston," I said.

Amman said, "Like a dream city."

The heart of the city did look shiny from a distance. Jim and I had uttered the same words when we drove into Houston from the East Coast.

Amman's gaze shifted to her gold bangles. "Things are bad right now. Air Force planes practice during the day and night. Even international flights have changed schedules. Everyone's expecting something terrible to happen with India. But I tell them, it won't happen now. Too many Americans on our soil." She rubbed her eyes. "But enough of that. I want to tell you about the family. All the cousins sent you love, especially Fazila. And your Shireen Khala, she made carrot halwa—you remember the special carrot sweet she used to make for you? I smuggled it in for you." Amman's mouth stretched into a smile, filling out her transparent cheeks. "You look well, Baita. Your... father... he would... have been proud to see you. And the children..."

I swallowed. After Abu's last heart attack, shortly before Jim and I moved to Houston, Amman had called me, begging me to return home. I told her that she should tell him to hold on, and that I would fly to see him. At the last moment, I changed my mind—as I always did whenever the question of returning to Karachi cropped up.

I turned down Rice Boulevard and entered our narrow street, greeted by shouts of teenagers who practiced basketball in one of the driveways. Amman nodded at the newly mown grass and at flowering crepe myrtles. "This is pretty, Baita. Your city's so much greener than I expected..."

The words "your city" grated on me. But she and I had not talked for a long time. Since leaving Karachi, I didn't feel as if I belonged to any city any more. My mouth was dry, and I yearned for a sip of lemon-water nimbu-paani to quench my thirst.

I pulled up along Mrs. Miller's driveway. She opened her red door as soon as I parked my car. Without waiting for me to turn off the car engine, Amman stepped out, and walked toward Mrs. Miller. She leaned forward, ready to kiss Mrs. Miller's cheek.

Clearly not used to this form of greeting, Mrs. Miller offered the right side of her face. "Delighted to meet you."

Behind her, the door swung open and Saira's bespectacled face and Sam's bright eyes appeared. Saira walked out, keeping her mouth closed to hide the new braces clamped around her teeth, but her younger brother ran up to the car to stand beside Mrs. Miller. Saira set a covered dish in the back seat.

"A pie I made to welcome you," said Mrs. Miller. "I hope you like dessert?"

Amman nodded, her eyes fixed on the children.

"Say hello to your Nani, children," I said in my answering machine voice. They mumbled inaudible words and twisted their hands and feet, staying close to Mrs. Miller. "This is Saira and this is Sam. I mean Sameer."

Sam frowned. He did not like being called his full name, and I remembered the arguments that Jim and I had when I insisted on Pakistani names for our children. Jim let me choose Saira because the pronunciation sounded close to 'Sara'—and that was what everyone called her. And as for Sameer, Jim and I had made a deal that Sameer's name would be shortened to Sam. I agreed that both children would use Ward, Jim's last name.

Pushing aside memories of early conflicts with my ex, I thanked Mrs. Miller and turned toward the car. Amman was already seated. Through my side vision, I caught a glimpse of her wiping her eyes with the edge of her sari. I knew she would not call Sameer 'Sam' and that she would pronounce Saira's name the correct way with an emphasis on the 'i. Amman was thinking about more than names. Surprised by the lump in my throat, I patted her hand. "It's going to take them time to get used to you."

She nodded, letting out a sniffle. She watched the children who stood outside the car, and her voice was muffled as if she had a cold. "Aren't they going to join us?"

"We live two houses away." I drove slowly as the children jogged beside us on the pavement, their backpacks bouncing.

Saira, tall for a ten-year-old, ran without glancing into the car. She kept her fingers pressed on her nose to stop her glasses from slipping, but Sam made faces at his reflection in the car window.

Inside, like a bird fluttering against glass, Amman's hands ran against the window, trying to find the button. When her window slid down, she leaned her face out. "Hello!"

Sam grinned and dropped to a slower pace as I pulled into our driveway, filled with the fragrance of star jasmine that I had recently replanted. Curly hair falling over her face, Saira opened the door for her grandmother. Sam walked up to Amman to stare up at her. She blinked back tears and pulled him close to her chest. His face smashed against Amman's frame, Sam grinned at me and rolled his eyes. Once she released him, he picked up her hand luggage with a shrug.

"Careful," Amman cautioned, her voice still sounding congested. She turned to me. "Baita, my suitcase is heavy. Can someone help?"

She was thinking of our Karachi house with its army of servants: cook, maid, gardener, gatekeeper, driver. Shaking my head, I grabbed her suitcase handle. "We'll manage."

Inside the house, Amman absorbed the hallway's potted palm, framed posters of art exhibits, and photographs of the children. I knew that her roving eyes were taking note of the early American oak dining set purchased in Newport, Connecticut, where Jim's parents lived. Only one framed mirror from Karachi hung on a wall; the remaining art—silver platters, Mughal miniature reproductions, and wall hangings—that Amman had sent me was in storage boxes.

I led her upstairs into Sam's bedroom, where she was to stay. A week ago, Saira and Sam had tossed a coin to see who would vacate a room. After losing, Sam adopted a refrain: "Why can't she stay in your studio? We'll put in a heater."

Amman, oblivious of the conflict that her visit caused, sank on the bed.

"You should take a nap." I was aware that I needed a break. "Or a shower? I'll let you know once dinner's ready."

She nodded. Stopping at the door, I watched her take off her shoes. From a distance, despite her height, she looked like a mannequin on the bed.

Feeling my gaze, Amman looked up. "Yasir should be here to meet your children."

I gripped the doorpost tighter. I understood all over again why I had stayed away all those years.

two

YASMEEN

I thumped down the stairs to the kitchen, battling tightness in my chest. Slamming a pot onto the stove didn't make me feel better. I poured Thai take-out into a container, and I dumped rice into another bowl. Smelling the curry, my cat Horace slinked around my legs, purring. The house was quiet with the children doing homework in Saira's room, for once not arguing for the television to be on.

I took advantage of the silence, and I wandered into my studio, the rarely used room adjoining the kitchen filled with unfinished canvases, tubes of paint, and an easel cradling an unpainted portrait of Saira. A long time ago, while spending our summer holidays at our Hawagali mountain home, Amman and I sketched and painted together. One day, sometime after Yasir and I turned thirteen, she stopped showing us her art, never telling us why. I kept up my drawing and painting, majoring in studio art at Tufts, but since graduating and moving to Houston, I, too, had given up my passion.

In my studio, I picked up objects as if they belonged to someone else: a rotary clock that Amman gave me before I left for college; a poster of my art show at Tufts when I got drunk on cheap champagne and slept with Jim for the first time; an exhibition catalog of the Persian miniatures exhibit at the Menil Collection shortly after we moved to Houston.

I paused. On the shelf in front of me sat a framed black and white photo. Yasir, wearing a dark sweater, his tall body folded into a curl and his toes sticking up to reveal dirt on his soles. His lips were split and his curly hair was alive with electricity. Smoke from his cigarette created a mist.

Yasir, my twin, older than me by seven minutes. We had been connected in all our thoughts, except on the night he died. Through my feverish body, I knew when he slipped on the patch of cobra plants, his ankle snapped, and his hands clawed on the roadside rocks. But on his last breath, my fever was high. I never knew his last moment. I never felt it.

I shot this slanted photo—with his head tilted and his crinkled eyes—when we turned seventeen. Here, on our secret hideout, the forbidden rooftop ledge, his face reminded me of the Happy Prince fairy tale, the one in which the gold-plated statue prince gave away his gold leaves to people who needed money. After his gold was gone, the townspeople said he was ugly, and they got rid of him.

Yasir and I read that story together. Upon reaching the end, his face reddened. "Why did they throw him away?" he demanded. "Wasn't his heart also made of gold? They gave him away because they couldn't see his heart? I'd never let them do that to me."

I hadn't thrown away Yasir's golden heart, but many years ago, since my college years—to avoid questions about him—I had wrapped his picture inside a black never-worn silk sari and set it inside a suitcase along with all my Pakistani cassettes, clothing, and books.

*   *   *

During the winter of 1982, just six months before Yasir leaves us forever, the country is in turbulence because the army has clamped down. Yasir, a pro at persuasion, manages to get Amman and Abu to allow us to take a trip with our older cousins, Aliya and Afshan, who are visiting from London. We are going into the heart of Sindh to see the 5,000-year-old ruins of Mohenjodaro. As we take off on the Fokker plane, we slap each other's hands in glee. We have never flown out of Karachi without our parents, and we are too young to be fearful of stories about desert bandits and violence; we can only celebrate Yasir's ability to create blind spots in other people's vision.

Once the plane lands in Mohenjodaro, the four of us wander through desert ruins. But the blazing sun melts our focus. When we try to board the plane to return to Karachi, we fumble in our pockets and purses, only to realize that we left our tickets at the rest house.

The airplane, already late, takes off without us, leaving us to spend the night at the rest house.

As dusk settles on the barren landscape, Yasir is like a bat, his energy and intellect recovered after sunset. He manages to charm some German archeologists to loan us their Range Rover jeep. We drive through flat dry sand, the landscape broken by brambles that cut into caked dirt. Once we reach the village, we navigate through streets and find an outdoor canteen. The owner produces platters of vegetables, omelets, kebabs, and daal that we consume without stopping. Satiated, we pile into the jeep. I take the wheel while Yasir reclines in the back seat, smoking. The sky glitters with stars. Far in the distance, a wolf's howl rumbles through the stillness.

Focused on driving, I am too tired to notice that the return journey to the rest house takes twice as long and that our path is bouncier. Only when I lower the beam do I see that I have driven away from the main road, and that we are driving on sand and brambles. Aliya scrambles to the front to join Afshan and me so they can study the map and guide me. Yasir remains in the back, listening to us argue over which way to turn to reach the rest house.

My attention switches to him when he sits up as if he heard a sound. I slow down. Through his ears, I hear bells jangle. Yasir sights a cow plodding in the sand. The moment I stop the jeep, Yasir leaps out onto the sand and races after the cow that only he can see. The bells still jangling in my ears, I shout, "Lead us Yasir!"

Yasir sprints in the dark, his eyes fixed on cattle, an entire herd, one that only he can see. A shrill whistle sounds and Yasir races toward a boy—whom I see through Yasir's eyes—wearing a white cotton tunic and waving a stick. I change the direction of the jeep and follow Yasir and the boy.

"Get back in!" Afshan yells at Yasir.

"Trust him," I mutter, knowing that the sisters are aware of even less.

Yasir continues to run in the dark, following the boy. From afar, we hear popping sounds like stones being hurled against tin roofs.

"Gunshots!" Aliya yells. "Yasir, get in!"

The jeep's engine is loud but steady like an air conditioner, but the popping sounds are shorter, like fireworks. I drive beside Yasir, trusting that the visions he sees will lead us to safety. In the dark, the stories that we read every day in the daily newspaper about masked gunmen kidnapping family members feel real, and our sprawling city at the edge of the desert feels far, as if it's located in another country.

Yasir slows down. I see a round hillock in the flat horizon. I slam the brakes. "It's the stupa!"

Looking to the right, we see lights from the rest house, which had been blocked by the rim of the Mohenjodaro stupa. Aliya clambers out of the jeep and I follow her, my arm around Yasir. The boy, the cows, the clanging of the cattle bell have vanished for Yasir, and the gunshots have dissipated, but Yasir's vision guided us to the ruins.

We step into the open ruins and walk through alleys. The moon rises over the horizon, bright like an autumn sun, shining on cobbled pathways. Around us, the ruins are alive with spirits we sensed earlier. I see a woman with her children, huddling in a doorway. The sizzle of onions fills the air. Chanting sounds emanate from the city center. For the first time through my own eyes, I glimpse Yasir's guide, the boy in the tunic, at one of the street corners.

We return to the hotel in silence, where the manager greets us, relieved that we are unharmed by bandits on the prowl. That night, I dream I am one of the women standing in a doorway. In the morning Yasir tells me that the dream ends with the boy and the woman becoming winged creatures that fly over the desert.

"The mother and son find their way to an island in the Arabian Sea," he tells me. "That's what they always wanted."

*   *   *

I replaced the photo on the shelf and used my shirt's lapel to wipe my cheek. Without Yasir, the magic in my life ended eighteen years ago. Every day, he and I had lived our own version of *A Thousand* and *One Nights*. When he left, I was alone, feeling as if my body, brain, and heart had been cut in half. With Yasir gone, I had lost the ending to my stories.

At the dinner table, the children polished off the saté, noodles, and curry. Saira and Sam were more quiet than usual. I could understand their confusion around Amman since I had never talked much about our family in Pakistan. All the relatives that they knew were from Jim's side and were scattered along the East Coast. Up until recently, neither child had asked many questions about Karachi.

I warmed Mrs. Miller's blueberry pie and brought it to the table. Saira followed me with vanilla ice cream, which she heaped on everyone's bowls.

"Mrs. Miller's such a great cook—enjoy," I said.

Not looking up, Amman toyed with the slice on her plate.

Saira licked her spoon. "Mrs. Miller's going to help me make cookies for Dad."

I placed another sliver of the pie on my plate. "You shouldn't let her overstrain herself." I turned to Amman. "She's great. I rarely get a baby-sitter—she's always there."

Amman concentrated on the landscape oil painting above my head.

"Her arthritis is serious, so some things are difficult for her. But she's so active. On 9/11, she was the first person at our door to ask how we were. Luckily, no one threatened us but her concern was thoughtful."

Amman placed a forkful of pie in her mouth. "Those must have been difficult times?"

"Yes and no." I glanced at the children and shook my head. I didn't want to talk about how—just a month ago—Saira had returned from school crying, telling me she wanted to go to another school because a group of fifth grade boys had snatched her sandwich and thrown it in the trash.

"Mom, why're they telling me to go back? Go where?" she had asked me, tears streaking down her cheeks.

I complained to the principal, and the boys were made to apologize to Saira. I wanted more action taken, but the principal excused the boys' behavior saying, "Everyone's traumatized by the events around the world. They don't know better."

Amman was still thinking about Mrs. Miller. "She has children of her own? Grandchildren?"

"In Iowa. Mrs. Miller visits them once a year."

"I see." Amman pushed away her plate. "I can't eat any more. Shall we have tea? I brought you a fresh box. Let me bring it downstairs?"

She returned with her arms full. "Since I was upstairs, I thought I'd bring more presents."

She handed me a floppy cotton cloth parcel, tied with a ribbon. I opened it to find a midnight blue silk sari with a green and purple border.

"I bought that in India five years ago," she said. Amman's parents had moved from north India before the 1947 Partition to the region that became Pakistan when her father had started a business in the northwest, supplying the British with army boots and clothing.

Saira slid her slender fingers—carbon copies of Amman's hands—over the material. "Mom, you should wear this. It's soft and pretty."

I nodded. I had not worn saris since I was a teenager, and I didn't know if I could any more.

Saira dropped to the carpet and pulled the tassels and tipped the velvet bag that Amman handed her. A silver necklace with a sapphire pendant fell on her palm. "Thank you, Nani!" Saira held up the necklace with two fingers.

A shrill whistle beckoned me to the kitchen where I searched for a suitable teapot, heated the milk, and found a strainer, noticing how the tea preparation ritual was still with me.

In the living room, Amman took a sip and nodded. "Excellent, Baita. You haven't lost your touch."

Surprised by the flash of pride I felt at her words, I held up my teacup as if it were a wineglass and we were toasting to her health.

Saira leaned back, the shift in her body causing the sapphire on her throat to sparkle. "This is cool, Nani. You should've waited till Christmas!"

Amman set her teacup down. "Christmas?"

"In two weeks. We usually fly up to see their father's family in Connecticut." I noticed that my voice was dry. "This year they'll be in town, so they'll go over to his place."

Sam collapsed on the sofa with his long legs curled under him, just as Yasir used to do. "There's a tree at Dad's place—right, Mom?"

I nodded and glanced at my watch. Even though I didn't enforce bedtime curfew like Amman used to, I liked the children to be in bed by nine—though their time seemed to have shifted since the divorce. Aware of Amman's gaze, I sent the children to brush their teeth, promising that I would be up to tuck them in bed soon.

"Amman, they do celebrate Christmas," I said as soon as the children left the room. "They'd feel strange at their school if they didn't."

"Do you celebrate our holidays with them?"

I shook my head. "You know that Muslim dates change each year. Besides, it's not as though we practiced much religion in Karachi." Yasir and I had never cared about Eid. We had our own communication, rituals, and language, which we expressed through dreams, glances, and smiles. And without my twin, I was incomplete.

three

LAILA

I spend another rainy day at home, dusting Yasmeen's studio and the living room, folding my clothes, and cooking chicken, potatoes, and lentils. Yasmeen's kitchen lacks spices from our part of the world, so I manage with garlic, onions, and crushed pepper. My cousins who live in an another part of Houston told me about a large South Asian population in Houston, and about stores that carry spices, curry leaves, halal goat meat, and much more. I wait for a weekend when Yasmeen is free, so she can drive me to the stores, after which I can cook a real meal for my family.

I hover by the doorway as the time for the children to return home from school approaches. Above, clouds bunch like angry frowns, and I jolt when thunder crashes. Heavy raindrops pelt the puddles in the driveway. A moment later, the school bus rounds the corner and the children step off the metal stairs. By the time Sameer enters, his body is soaked. He has been playing in the rain. I cringe. In my grandson's long face and curly hair, I see too many reminders of my son's final moments in Hawagali.

"The playground's flooded!" cries Sameer.

"You should not play in the rain!" I try to soften my voice. "Your mother's told you that?"

Saira and Sameer exchange looks. I can tell that they have trouble understanding why I, the Nani they have never met before can feel free to scold them. But they don't know the dangers that storms can bring.

"You can catch a cold and something bad can happen." I don't know how much Yasmeen has shared with her children about their uncle.

I lead Sameer into the bathroom to dry out his hair with Yasmeen's hair dryer. We are in the kitchen when a loud bang, like several gunshots at once, goes off outside. The ceiling light flickers and lights fade, submerging the house in the storm's purple light.

"What's going on?" says Saira. Her eyes, hidden behind her glasses, are more distant than usual. "It's too dark. I don't like it."

I don't like darkness either, but I try to remain calm for the children's sake. With their help, I round up two candles, light a fire in the study, and am trying to locate the electric company's phone number when Mrs. Miller telephones us to say that a main transformer has broken down and that the electricity will be restored in a few hours.

Candles are lit when the phone rings again: Yasmeen is at her office and wants to make sure that the children are home and safe.

"I'm stuck at my office," she says. "The streets are flooded. Could you prepare their dinner and make sure that they get to bed on time? I'll be home as soon as I can."

In Karachi, electric breakdowns happen all the time, but this one, mixed with a thunderstorm, frightens me. I pick up my knitting while Saira and Sameer remain close to the window, their noses pressed to the glass. I know they are waiting for their mother—even though she has told them that the water won't recede for a few hours. The whirling siren of an ambulance cuts through the sound of water descending from the skies. Another clap of thunder sets off a car alarm. The rain's trickle changes to rattling. Sameer yanks open the front door to find hail, the size of small marbles, bouncing on the driveway and thumping against the neighbor's roof and the garage door.

"Stay inside," I say, my voice competing with the hail clatter.

"Mom doesn't like the rain." He turns around and rolls his eyes at me but does not leave the doorway. "Why isn't she home?"

"She's waiting until the storm ends." I need to distract the children—and myself. Worry becomes a mist that wraps around me. "Has anyone shown you how to make animal shadows?" I hold up my fingers against the candle flame to make a deer-shaped shadow. I bob the shadow towards Sameer. Neither child turns around. I try again. "Would you like to hear a story?"

"You can't read in candlelight," Saira says without leaving the window.

"I remember hail from the summer when I was ten years old." I raise my voice to compete with a thunder crash. "Every year, my family motored to Hawagali, a hill station in north Pakistan. Hawagali is a beautiful place with forests and fresh water streams—"

I hear the front door click shut. Sameer moves closer. Paying little attention to him or to Saira, I continue talking as if to the cat curled by my feet:

*   *   *

Our mountain house was large and rambling, with verandah wooden lattices so old that they looked as if they would dissolve if we touched them. Our lawn was grassy with sprawling bushes, perfect for the hide-and-seek that my brothers, sister, and I played. In Hawagali, my siblings and I had to follow two rules: First, we weren't allowed to leave the building grounds without adults, and second, we weren't allowed to talk to strangers. We were told that children were kidnapped from the mountainside and were taken to beggar camps, where their arms or legs were cut off. Others were blinded. After maiming them, the kidnappers took the children to cities and forced them to beg.

The grownups repeated these rules to us every year. But my sister Shireen and I broke both rules during the summer that I turned ten.

We had guests staying with us—my cousin Babur and his parents. We didn't know them well since they lived abroad. Babur, sixteen, tall, with a voice deep like a man's, was the same age as my brothers, but he rarely joined their cricket games. Instead, he kept to himself, often disappearing for hours with his air gun strapped to his shoulder as if he carried a hunting rifle.

One evening, a hailstorm began, after which we were pelted by rain for a full week. Temperatures dipped lower, and we spent our summer evenings huddled by the fireside. Shireen and I drew in our coloring books while our older brothers played cards or listened to the radio. Never social, Babur skulked in his bedroom, a small section in the attic, which had been closed off to create a room.

One afternoon, Shireen and I played shipwreck in the open area of the attic. I leapt on a wooden chest and was about to slash Shireen's head off with my pretend-saber, when Babur came up the stairs on his way to his room.

He paused at his door. "Beware of kaneezes," he hissed.

Shireen and I dropped our weapons. "Kaneez? She's in 'Pindi." We were talking about our maid, Kaneez Bua, who was young, but known for her grouchiness.

Babur shrugged. "Don't you know that in Hawagali a witch is called kaneez? The kaneezes here hang off trees like bats. They wear black robes."

I pictured Kaneez Bua in her gray burqa, who lived with family in 'Pindi, and I remembered her stern eyes and her clipped voice telling me to sit still while she pulled knots out of my hair. She never seemed to care if she hurt me—I could understand why, in the mountains, her name meant 'witch.'

Babur thrust his face so close to mine that I could see hair stubble on his cheek. "Kaneezes don't like little girls. They swoop down and tear earrings off your earlobes. Sometimes they enter the attic." He snorted. "You don't believe me? Wait till one gets you. You'll know she's close if you smell stinky breath or see yellow eyes."

Shireen and I looked around the attic, half-expecting to see a woman who looked like Kaneez Bua swinging off the ceiling beams.

Babur disappeared into his bedroom, closing the door behind him. A second later, he stuck his head out of the door again. "And oh, don't go near those poisonous cobra plants. They're evil, too." He shut the door with a click.

Shireen and I knew about cobra plants that grew along the mountainside. In early summer, cobra plants were green, but towards August, the plants grew tall and purple, their striped long leaves ending with thin thread that quivered like snakes' tongues past the leave's tips. Even before Babur said anything about them, Shireen and I had avoided the plants, but after hearing his pronouncement, we promised each other never to touch a cobra plant again. And though I didn't believe Babur's stories, I took off my earrings and hid them inside the chest of drawers that my sister and I shared.

*   *   *

"That's kind of scary, Nani," Saira interrupts. "I mean it's weird to have stories about witches. I always read that stuff in books. But the story didn't really happen, did it?"

I pat her shoulder. "Well, we were young. The story felt real to us. Do you want to hear what happens next?"

*   *   *

A few days later, the sun shone as if rain had never passed through our surroundings. Shireen and I were so happy to be outside that we forgot Babur's words. We began to play a catch game, and when Shireen threw our ball over the boundary wall, we stepped outside the gate without thinking. After searching along the roadside with little success, we gave up and started playing running-catching. Before we could register that we had broken family rules, our house was out of sight.

Shireen said, "We should just go to Titlipark."

Titlipark, a few miles up on a mountaintop—with its log cabin, trees to climb, and wild monkeys—was our favorite picnic spot in Hawagali. I agreed, knowing the grownups were napping and that we wouldn't be missed. We chased each other along the uphill road, racing between pigeons that bathed in puddles. Deeper in the forest, wild strawberries winked and monkeys screamed. After walking uphill for half an hour, we were out of breath. We slowed down. Titlipark had never seemed far when we walked with everyone else.

The sun sank behind pine trees and tree shadows lengthened, reminding me of warnings we had been given about kidnappers and beggar camps. I thought of the city, where throngs of beggar children pressed wet cheeks to automobile windows. Some children didn't have tongues or eyes; others were missing legs or arms. I shivered.

I remembered Babur's story about witches who looked like Kaneez Bua, and I was glad that I wasn't wearing my earrings. When I stared at a fir tree, the trunk seemed to have transformed into a moving object who looked like Kaneez Bua approaching us with her burqa flapping around her like wings. Shireen pulled at my sleeve, pointing to the mountainside where spilling, swarming, and coiling around fir tree trunks, were cobra plants that seemed to have come alive. We screamed and sprinted downhill, certain that the eyes and necks of cobra plants were following us down the road, and that a kaneez was hot on our trail.

From out of the mist, appeared an old man, wearing a tweed hat with gray hair that sprouted in all directions. His shadow was crooked, making him look like a puppet. The man stretched his cane across our path to stop us. "Hello, girls," he said. "Is everything okay?"

I grabbed Shireen's hand.

"Where's your mother?" the man asked, his deep voice sounding like a growl.

"Leave us alone!" I stammered.

His eyebrows shot up to join tufts of hair growing beneath his cap. "You had better come with me," he said, reaching for my free hand. Shireen recovered and kicked the man's shin. We grabbed each other's hands and raced into the mist, stopping only once we were certain that the man was not behind us. Our hearts pounded, our eyes bulged, and our feet hurt.

"Is he gone?" Shireen asked.

I swallowed, sensing danger not yet past in the moonless night with few stars sparkling through the web of mist. Fireflies blew between us. The scent of crushed pine mingled with mist and earth rose to our nostrils. In the trees above, an owl hooted and leaves rustled. A shriek, belonging to neither animal nor person, speared the air.

Shireen's cold hands clutched my elbow. "What was that?" she quavered.

I shook my head. We heard a flapping sound. Above us, a dark shadow with black wings that spanned more than six feet flew from tree to tree.

"Run!" we screamed. Our footsteps thumped on the downhill road. We could feel rustling above us. Fear of the kaneez spurred us to run faster than we ever had before. In the distance, through the fog, we sighted our house lights inviting us to safety. Rounding the corner, we passed the entrance lampposts, and our feet crunched the gravel on our driveway.

Shireen pushed the front door open. Once inside, she slammed it shut. A thump sounded against the door.

Our parents emerged from the study, their foreheads wrinkled with worry. When we told them that we had tried to walk to Titlipark, their fear was replaced with anger. Shireen and I listened without saying a word.

Inwardly, I resolved never to stray outside again. The flapping, the shriek, the old man, and the cobra plants were enough to make me believe Babur's stories about the haunted mountainside. I barely slept that night. When I did, my rest was haunted by a scream and by dark shadows that followed us. I was certain the man was a kidnapper, and that Shireen and I had been marked as targets by kaneezes that roamed the mountainside.

*　*　*

I pause to see the children's mouths dropped open. "Wow, Nani," Sameer says. "They must've grounded you."

I move around the room, lighting more candles. I am glad that the storm is fading. "Yes. We were punished."

"Did you see witches?" Sameer asks.

*　*　*

The next day was sunny and our entire family went to Titlipark for a picnic, but Shireen and I had to stay at home with my older aunt. We slumped in the dark stairwell, arguing over who had made the decision to leave the grounds.

A deep voice spoke from behind us. "Stop grumbling! First you break rules. Then you fuss!"

I whipped my head around. "Babur! You didn't go with them!"

Babur grinned, showing his wolf teeth. "Of course not. I'm going to shoot kaneezes."

"Shoot kaneezes?" I thought of Kaneez Bua squatting in the open courtyard at our house, scrubbing our clothes or crushing garlic and ginger, her sleeves rolled up and her face gleaming with sweat. I felt sorry for her, but Babur gave me little time to think. He signaled for us to follow him, which we did, all the while thinking about how Babur was paying attention to us for the second time. Once in the attic, we told him about the old man and the black shadow.

Babur nodded as if he already knew. "That was a kaneez following you. And the man must have been a kidnapper. I'm glad you weren't harmed. Those cobra plants are dangerous. They wrap around children's legs and trip them so the kaneezes can catch them."

My eyes must have widened because Babur said: "Don't worry. I'm going to destroy the kaneezes!" He locked the attic door behind him, closing out the previous night's dangers, and pulled open the curtains to allow speckled sunlight to enter past pine trees.

Babur inserted shiny steel pellets into his gun's chamber and issued orders: "You have to be quiet. Signal to me by raising your left hand if you think we're being watched by a kaneez."

The windows were open without glass or bars. When I crouched close to the one he assigned me to watch, I couldn't stop thinking about how easily a kaneez could fly inside. Ten minutes later, Shireen raised her left hand. Moving near her window, I saw a dark shadow hanging off the oak tree-branch, but its cloudy shape was unclear. Babur inched closer. He rested the air gun's nozzle on the windowsill and pulled the trigger.

Ping. The bullet ricocheted off a chimney. We heard flapping and saw a shadow flying upwards; its dark shape made me want to run downstairs and hide in my bed.

"Missed. Next time I'll get it. Do you know that a kaneez becomes harmless when I shoot it? The witch turns into a monkey, a squirrel, or a crow. You'll see."

For a long time, nothing happened. The heat knocked us into a doze, but when a shadow flew across my face, I opened my eyes. I saw a kaneez flapping her wings past the oak branches. A thick smell like raw sewage filled the air. Yellow eyes pierced into mine, making my heart pound so hard that I was certain the beat could be heard at the valley tea shop.

My chest tight, I slithered close to Babur and pinched his arm. Awakening with a jolt, he saw my left hand raised. He picked up his air gun, took aim, and pulled the trigger.

Something small, like a rock, crashed and hurtled, breaking the tree's boughs. We popped our heads over the windowsill, sunlight blinding us, but the shadow had disappeared. Instead, far below, on the very lowest branches of the oak tree, a crow stretched its wings—the kaneez transformed.

Babur put away his gun and said, "One less kaneez to contend with!"

*　　*　　*

I set my needles down and clap my hands. Sameer and Saira slump on the carpet, their mouths slack. "And that's how that story ends."

Sameer sits up. "Wait—what happened next?"

"After that first afternoon, Shireen and I spent many hours in the attic room, keeping watch for him as he shot at dark shadows in the trees. By the time summer ended, Babur was sure we had destroyed all the kaneezes. We said good-bye to him, and returned to our house in 'Pindi."

"But—" Sameer frowned. "Were those witches real? And what about the cobra plants? And that woman who worked at your house—did she die or something?"

I laugh. "I can't tell you all my stories in one night, can I?"

"Come on, Nani!"

Saira speaks up. "I didn't like the part about the beggars."

I bend down and draw her close to me. "It's only a story, dear." Saira leans against me and my heartbeat increases; this is the first time Saira has been close to me. I tuck her hair behind her ears and kiss her forehead. Her gray eyes—lost amidst purple plants and yellow-eyed witches in Pakistan's northern mountains—drift far from me, but she reaches up and kisses my cheek.

Just then, electric lights flicker, and power returns as suddenly as it faded. The television screen lights up, and the refrigerator hums.

"Time for bed," I say.

Saira and Sameer dance around the room blowing out candles. Long after I tuck them in bed and kiss them goodnight, I lie in the dark, waiting for Yasmeen to return. Outside, the wind drops, and branches brush against unbarred windows.

The children are asleep by the time the garage door rumbles to let in Yasmeen's car. I hear the side door open and click. In Yasmeen's house, sounds echo. Homes are different from those I know: Our Pakistani houses have more hallways and activity. At night, guests drop by, and servants wash dishes or talk outside beneath trees, listening to Indian film songs.

This kind of silence reminds me of 'Pindi where we returned after Yasir passed away. Kaneez Bua—who worked in our family and took care of Yasmeen and Yasir when we spent time in 'Pindi—didn't sleep on the floor on her roll-down bedding. Instead, she sat on her haunches beside Yasmeen's bed, holding her hand till she fell asleep.

In the morning, Kaneez Bua's stern face was soft; her burqa hung on a peg in the kitchen where it remained for the next few days as she joined in the soyem prayers to mourn Yasir's departure.

four

YASMEEN

"We had fun last night," Sam said. He stirred frosted flakes in his cereal bowl, creating a splatter on his tablemat.

"Don't play with your food!" I barked. "What did you do without electricity?" Morning sunrays streamed through the window, making us feel as if the previous night's storm had never occurred, especially since electricity had been restored by the time I reached home. My fellow workers and I had to spend four hours at the office waiting for water to recede from nearby I-10.

"Nani told us a story. In the dark. It was cool."

I turned around to unload the dishwasher. "A story?"

Saira spoke up. "About a place called Ha—Hawa—"

"Hawagali." I finished the sentence for her.

Saira nodded. "The story was about witches. And how her cousin made the witches go away—"

"I know the story," I said. "Don't you both need to hurry up, so you don't miss your bus?" Yasir and I used to throw pebbles into trees so we could see crows fly and squirrels scamper. Transformed kaneezes, we tagged them just as Amman and Shireen Khala had twenty years before us.

Sam picked up his backpack. "Know what I want on my birthday?"

I braced myself.

"An air gun. Like Nani's cousin, you know?"

After walking the children to the bus, I returned to the house and chugged more coffee. Silly of me to think that Amman could visit and avoid talking about Hawagali or about Yasir. Hawagali was where she had spent so much of her childhood, Yasir was her son, and storytelling was her gift. When I sent Amman the invitation to visit Houston, I had not thought about how her presence would affect me. Back then, wilting in post-divorce loneliness, I had acted on a passing whim.

I sorted through my documents and found the detergent campaign report that was due in the afternoon, forcing myself to push away memories that crowded upon me. I jumped when I heard tap water surge behind me. Amman, fresh from her shower, filled the kettle with water.

I snapped my briefcase shut. "Would you like breakfast?"

"Don't worry, Baita. I'll find something when I'm ready."

Amman looked rested, which was more than I could say for myself. "I'll be late again today. Do you mind taking care of the children's dinner? Mrs. Miller's already in Iowa." I hated my formal tone, but talking was better than smashing my coffee cup against the wall. I never stayed at work so late, and one of my favorite Wednesday afternoon activities was to watch the kids practice soccer at school. I had cluttered my days with appointments and—if I wanted to be honest with myself—I would admit that I was not ready to spend time with Amman. At least the children would be with their Nani, I reasoned with myself. But my guilt, like cough syrup, remained coated on my tongue.

Oblivious to the noise in my head, Amman smiled. "The children are no trouble." She opened her phone diary. "You know how your Khadija Phophi phoned me? I was wondering if I could see her. Where can I find out about buses?"

In the weeks prior to Amman's arrival, I had talked to more relatives around the US than I had over the last ten years. "A bus where? Indianapolis?"

"Is that far?" Amman flipped through the pages of her diary. Slips of paper—scribbled phone numbers and names in the US, Greece, and Australia, written in Urdu and in English—floated to the floor.

I collected her papers. "Far," I said, resurfacing.

She raised her eyebrows.

Sam's geography book lay on the table. Flipping the pages to a

US map, I traced my finger from Houston to Indianapolis. "About the same distance from Houston that Karachi is from 'Pindi."

"So it's not a day trip." Her voice faltered. "I don't like flying... I suppose I won't meet Khadija. And I won't have time to see anyone on the New York side either, but how about Bano?" She showed me a penciled address.

I sighed. If I didn't leave soon, I would be late. "Oregon is even further from here than California." Amman was armed with telephone numbers and addresses of every relative in the US.

"I always forget how big America is." She turned more pages. "I should at least pay a visit to Safia. Isn't she in Texas? I could take care of one visit before the children's holidays start?"

I placed my coffee mug in the sink. "That might work. Brenham's an hour away."

Amman's face brightened. "I'll telephone her. Perhaps they can pick me up. I won't ask you to drive me. I know you're busy."

Pushing away my guilt, I headed for the door.

A few puddles gathered along the streets, but most of the rainwater had drained away or evaporated. A couple of abandoned cars on each side of the 610 Loop were evidence that flooding had occurred. I reached the office late, but the parking lot lay empty. Pulling in beside my friend Janet's car, I grabbed my briefcase and entered the office-house. Inside, the phone rang, but our receptionist Nancy was not at her desk.

George, a colleague, breezed by. He thrust his chin in the direction of Nancy's chair. "She'll be out. House flooded. They still don't have power."

Despite the problems the storm had caused in parts of the city, my morning remained unchanged, packed with client calls, a business lunch, more meetings to review accounts, and a planning discussion for the detergent campaign. Close to five, finally free, I threw off my shoes and dropped in my chair. Just as I had predicted—or planned—I would have to stay late to get the report done.

Taking a deep breath, I sorted through emails, letters, magazines, junk mail, aware of my mind wandering to Amman. She must be bored with her Houston routine, especially since her life in Karachi—with streams of visitors, running errands for older family members, and volunteer work at the school where she had taught art—was so different. After Yasir's death, Amman had begun standing up to Abu.

And instead of being Karachi's number one socialite, she became a celebrated community worker, visiting hospitals and schools. In Houston, she distracted herself by reading, cooking, and waiting for the children and me to return home. With Amman still in my thoughts, I turned the pages of a home decoration magazine. I could phone her to see how her day was going. I stopped short.

A pink phone message —*Please call Carlos*— dated three days ago sat between magazine sheets. My hand jostled my coffee mug, making it teeter and fall to one side. Coffee dregs spattered the front of my linen skirt. I raced to the bathroom to scrub the stain before it started living on the fabric. I knew that he would call, but I wasn't prepared for the rush of blood from my chest to my cheeks.

My friend Janet stepped out of her room as I passed her office. "Can you take a moment and visit me? I want to show you something." She caught my arm and pulled me toward the image on her computer. A juice bottle, taller than a giraffe, leaned against a red rhododendron bush with the backdrop of a rainforest. "What do you think?" she asked. "Does that work?"

I looked over her shoulder. "I suppose..."

"What's wrong?" Janet, my friend for almost a decade, could tell when I was upset. She and I had met after Jim and I moved to Houston when I started working at the advertising agency where Janet held a graphics director position. From Trinidad, she had studied in British schools as I had before arriving in the US. Tall, narrow-waisted, Janet was composed, a contrast to me, always in a hurry.

"Nothing. I've had one hell of a day. Now I'm staying late to redo this damn report for Henrietta."

"Your mom's by herself?" Janet could never understand how I had cut myself off from home. She visited her family once each year and telephoned her mother every other day. Of course, all Pakistani families that I knew kept in touch with relatives. Some had brought entire households, including cooks and maids, to live with them.

"Yes—she's helping with the kids. I just found a three-day-old message. From Carlos."

"He's back?"

Years ago, Janet and her husband Tony had introduced me to Carlos, a history professor at the university, and she was the first person I told about my affair with Carlos. The liaison lasted for a few weeks, and Carlos and I managed to remain friends, even while Jim and I became more distant.

"Apparently so."

She prodded my shoulder. "Relax. So what? You don't have to sleep with him every time you see him. Or maybe you're worried you won't! You going to call him back?"

"Don't know yet..."

I gave Janet a hug, and returned to my room to settle at my desk, trying to block the office manager's conversation with a temp. "Come on, let me buy you dinner! It's Friday night. What else you got happenin'?" He laughed.

The temp giggled. "I don't know... I've been warned about you!"

Resisting the urge to tell them to take their flirtation elsewhere, I turned my attention to the report.

The last time that I had seen Carlos was six months earlier, when we ran into each other in Phoenix, the week after my divorce finalized, and Jim returned from Costa Rica with Molly, his main squeeze.

*   *   *

My Saturday brownie-making morning is disrupted by my phone's vibration. The number shows up as belonging to Henrietta, my boss. I lick the batter to pick up the phone.

"You'll need to go to a conference in Phoenix," Henrietta announces.

By the time I muster up words to inform her that I need time to consider her offer, Henrietta has hung up. I call Janet, begging her to take my place.

"You should go," Janet responds. "You can use the conference as time for yourself!"

Two weeks later, Jim takes the children for the weekend, and I board the plane to Phoenix. As the stewardess serves orange juice and snacks, I'm conscious of my pulse beating at the base of my neck. Exiting the airport, I settle into the cab, my breath racing fast as if someone were pressing my accelerator while I stand still. The out-of-breath feeling remains as I check into the hotel room, shower, and change. Dashing out of the elevator to attend the opening session of the conference, I collide into someone in an equal hurry. Carlos.

"What're you doing here?" I exclaim. A couple of weeks ago, we had seen each other in Houston and Carlos mentioned that he would be flying to Guatemala for six months.

He grins. "If we were in a grocery store, I'd say it was the habit of Ríos men to plow down women," he says, rubbing his shoulder, referring to a story he told me about how his father fell in love with his mother after bumping into her with a grocery cart in a San Francisco store. He sweeps me in a hug and tells me he's in town to meet the co-author of a book they are writing. "I leave for Guatemala after my meeting," he adds. "We were meant to intersect before I vanish into Mayan country."

After I complete my conference meetings, Carlos and I rent a car and drive to South Mountain Park, where we hike to the top of the trail. Hawks circle the cloudless blue sky. Standing atop a red boulder, I open my arms to pull the sky into my chest.

Carlos laughs. "Come with me to Guatemala! We'll hike every day."

I meet his eyes, aware that my smile stretches broader than sunlight on the horizon at dawn.

By twilight, we return to the base and drive toward the city via a back road. Evening sun rays cast gold and red splashes on cacti and rocks, while shots of purple streak the sky. Carlos places his warm hand on top of my knee. I intertwine our fingers. Pulling over to the side of the road, Carlos turns to kiss me. We fling ourselves on the back seat of the rented Chevy. No cars pass and there are no interruptions. Afterwards, realizing that we're still wearing our hiking socks, we laugh. "Too much trouble!" I say, buttoning my shirt.

We spend that night in my hotel room. Lying between cool sheets, with Carlos' chest brushing against mine, I know once again what it feels like to be alive.

The following afternoon at my departure gate, Carlos crosses his arms. "Who's going to meet you in Houston?"

"My car's parked there."

"I'd be there to pick you up if I could..."

I meet his dark eyes. "That would be nice."

*   *   *

I tapped my fingers on the stacks of paper beside my computer. Carlos did send me emails from Guatemala City, urging me to join him, but I never wrote back and the emails stopped. For those weeks in July—the kids were at their first sleepaway summer camp and Jim and I were officially divorced—I ended up jogging each evening around Memorial Park and picking up take-out from downtown Houston's Vietnamese restaurants. I kicked myself for not joining Carlos on his jaunt, but by the time I was ready, he had already begun working at the university. My three weeks alone reminded me of my first semester at Tufts—before I discovered pot, wine, and my wild friend Sarah—when I lived in a wooden library carrel and wrote letters to my dead twin, which I tore up into one-centimeter scraps that I carried back to my dorm to discard in my own trash can.

Outside my office, people called good night to each other, cars started and drove off, making me wish that I, too, were somewhere else. I had joined the marketing agency after Sam started going to kindergarten, because Jim thought working full-time would be a great way to stop me from "moping around the house" as he saw it. I agreed. My paintings weren't selling, and I was stagnating at home. The best thing to come of the job was my friendship with Janet.

Henrietta's tight-lipped face appeared at my doorway, her red nails smears of blood on the wall.

"Jasmine, are you working on that report?" Her eyebrows merged into her silver hairline.

My shoulders tensed. After years of working with her, Henrietta still insisted on mispronouncing my name.

"Be a dear, will you, and drop it off at my house in the morning?" Her tone was questioning, but after years with her, I knew she was issuing an order. She ducked out of the doorway, her heels clicking on the wooden floor.

I pounded my keyboard, knowing that my Saturday would be consumed by the drive to the southwest corner of Houston's unending suburbia. Two hours later, I stood up to stretch and glimpsed myself in the window. My face looked long and my curly hair drooped. I picked up the phone and dialed home.

Amman reported that the children had eaten dinner, finished their homework, and were watching television. "I phoned your cousin Safia," she added. "Since she's free, I'll go see her on Sunday night for a few days... I said Sunday because I thought it might be more convenient for you to take me to the bus-stop?"

"That sounds fine." I doodled eyebrows on a scratch piece of paper. A faint knocking sounded on my door making me glance at my watch. It was late and no one else but the guard should have been around.

On the other end, Amman was still talking. "Shall I keep some dinner out for you?"

The rap sounded again. "Don't worry about dinner. I'll pick up something on the way home. Please give the children my love."

"Baita, don't work so hard!" Amman's voice was urgent.

I replaced the phone on its cradle and opened the door.

In the hallway, grinning like a pirate discovering plunder, stood Carlos.

five

LAILA

"Was that Mom?" asks Saira, breaking away from her Harry Potter book.

"She'll be home soon."

Sameer presses a finger on the remote and lowers the volume. "It's so boring. We don't even have cable. You didn't have TV when you were little, Nani. What did you do?"

I smile. "We played games. And had adventures."

Sameer pins his eyes on the television screen to watch an advertisement where a wrestler in shiny blue underclothes smashes a man to the ground. "What kind of adventures?"

"Like the one in Hawagali."

I also have Saira's attention. "Did you ever see those witches again?"

Sameer lowers the television volume. "I want a ghost story!"

*   *   *

Close to our Hawagali house was a sunken park that looked like a giant's grassy bowl. Stone steps led to the park's base that was filled with swings, a seesaw, a jungle gym, and a steel slide that felt cold to our bottoms. The park's slopes were freckled with buttercups, sun-centered daisies, and dandelions, and we sometimes rolled down the

43

incline. On the street, across from the park, stood a double-storied abandoned house. We were told that English people once used to live there, but that they left a long time ago even before Pakistan gained independence.

Sometimes, before turning toward the stairs of our park, Shireen and I stopped in front of the two-storied house. Though the front windows were boarded up, the grass of the front lawn was never overgrown. We would imagine white-gowned women standing on the grass as they leaned on their parasols, but the building was daunting. It was constructed with dark wood, and even from the street, we could see that its front door was caked with dirt. Some days, when we felt brave, we would tiptoe to a barred glass window on the side and try to peer inside, but could never see anything because the glass had not been cleaned for years.

One afternoon, as Shireen and I rode the seesaw in the park, we noted that crows' cawing had increased. We were alone except for our ayah-nanny Nasreen, who was combing her hair. More crows circled above us, so Shireen and I decided to investigate what was happening. The afternoon's mist made the park and the street dark and mysterious. Holding hands, Shireen and I stepped into the cloud. When the cloud parted, we stood in front of the dark house. But this time, its front door was flung open.

And on the lawn, stood a woman in a white gown, crumbling bread and feeding crows. A man's dark face appeared at the front door. A cloud rolled in, blocking the sunlight. When the mist cleared, the woman and man had vanished. Even the crows had flown away.

I shook Shireen's arm. "Did you see that?"

As if awakening from a dream, Shireen rubbed her eyes. "I think so—"

From the park below, we heard Nasreen calling for us. Shireen and I raced down the stairs, uncertain how to interpret what we had seen. But after that day, each time we walked toward the park, we stopped in front of the double-storied house. I felt my heartbeat increase, but the man and the woman did not reappear.

One day, Shireen was in a bad mood. On our way to the park, she said, "I think the woman was just our imagination. Babur's stories were fake, too!" She turned around and ran back to our house.

I couldn't understand my sister's anger. Instead of following her home as I would have done other times, I continued toward the park with Nasreen. I wasn't going to let my sister spoil my afternoon. One of Nasreen's friends sat at a bench, waiting for her. The women started to gossip. I climbed to the top of the slide and sat there, humming and ignoring the coldness on my behind. If Shireen could be uncaring, so could I.

Sunlight shifted as a cloud rolled in, blowing in a gust of wind. Crows cawed. As sunlight filtered through clouds, I noticed a flock of crows converging above the stairs. The sun slipped away again. I slithered down the slide. "I'll be back in a moment," I called to Nasreen.

Too busy talking to her friend, Nasreen didn't look up. I ran up the stairs and walked into a cold wet cloud, so dark that I could barely see. I clenched my fists and stepped forward. Fog parted, revealing the house and a flickering light. I headed toward the light. The cawing of the crows was muffled. As sunlight cut through the clouds, I realized that I had crossed the street and stood at the entrance of the old house.

Like an actress in a black and white movie, the white-gowned woman stood on the lawn, scattering naan-bread for the crows. She turned around to meet my eyes. Part of me wanted to race back to the park, while another part of me wanted proof to show Shireen that the woman existed. Pushing away the worry that the woman might be a kaneez feeding crows to transform them to witches again, I stepped forward.

My fear vanished when she smiled at me. A dark face, belonging to a boy my age, hid behind the woman's skirt. Keeping her eyes fixed on me, the woman floated forward.

"Hello, dear," she said. Her voice had the lilt of someone who had lived in our country for a long time. "My name is Alice Khan and this is my son, Rustam."

I remembered my family's rule about not talking to strangers, but I couldn't resist Alice's charm. I also liked that her son was named after a Persian mythical king. "Hello," I replied.

Alice laughed. "I have seen you playing with your sister. Sometimes you ride by on your horses. Is your sister—she is your sister, correct? She's not with you today?"

I shook my head.

"Might you be interested in trying my fruitcake?"

Rustam held out a red toy train engine with yellow wheels.

"That's pretty!" I said. "Can I touch it?"

He ducked behind his mother's skirt again, but peered around her to say, "I have the whole train set. Want to see?"

I loved toy cars and trains and had never seen such intricate toys. I knew that I should return to the park and inform Nasreen about what I was doing, but I was afraid that by the time I returned, Alice and Rustam would have vanished. I nodded.

Alice smiled. "Let's go in."

I followed them inside the house to a hallway, where lit candles explained the gleam that I had seen through the mist. Rustam pointed to a steep staircase on the side and invited me to join him. We entered another hallway with multiple doors. Rustam thrust open one of the doors. We entered his bedroom, where his bed was pushed to the side. Train tracks zigzagged on the floor, ducked beneath a table, and meandered toward the center. Miniature guards and coal men stood in the last carriage. I dropped to the floor and watched Rustam fasten the engine in his hand to one of the carriages.

"The ones in front are passenger cars," he said. "My father made them. He's the best craftsman in the world."

I remembered the dark-faced man that Shireen and I had glimpsed. "Where is he? Your father?"

Rustam did not answer me. Instead, he stood up and walked out of the room, leaving me feeling as if a cloud had rolled between us. I followed him into the kitchen where Alice had laid out a white china set. She cut me a slab of fruitcake and poured tea in teacups with lips so thin that I felt as if I were drinking from air. As we chatted, I looked outside to notice that the sun was descending behind the mountains.

"I must return to the park," I said. "They're going to worry about me..."

"Wait," Rustam said. He ran out of the room and reappeared with a purple engine in one hand and a passenger car in the other. "For you," he said.

I shook my head. "No. They match your train set."

"Please. I have two engines. I need only one." He thrust the cars toward me. I didn't know what would be ruder: to refuse or to accept. Lifting up my hands and depositing the train cars in my open palms, Rustam decided for me.

"Thank you," I said. I shook their hands and bade my hosts good-bye.

"Come by and visit!" Alice waved.

I stepped inside a cloud. The sun disappeared, and I felt eyes upon my back. Looking up, I shivered. Yellow eyes watched me from low branches of a pine tree. A kaneez.

At the park, Nasreen scolded me a little, but she had been so absorbed in her conversation that she had not noticed how long I had been gone. On the walk home, I held the engine in my pocket to confirm that my tea-visit had really occurred. I remembered the yellow eyes on the tree branches, and I didn't know how to understand new friendships against lurking danger. I wished Babur could be present to explain everything.

Over dinner, I ignored Shireen, but at bedtime, when she and I retired to our room, I placed my new toys on my bedside table.

"Where did you get those?" Shireen asked, forgetting that she and I weren't speaking to each other. Only after she promised to accept every word of my story, did I pour out my adventure with Alice and Rustam.

The next day, on our walk to the park, Shireen and I tried to enter the house again through the front door, but it was locked and jammed with dirt as if it had not been opened for a while.

Shireen's eyebrows pulled close together. "Are you sure you entered through this doorway?"

I was close to tears. "I was here yesterday! A boy named Rustam did show me his train set and he did give me that purple carriage." I picked up the lion-faced door knock and pounded its brass plate. No one answered. I slumped on the doorstep. "They were nice. And the cake was delicious!"

Shireen sat beside me and put her arms around my shoulder. "Maybe they aren't home."

I knew that she was trying her best to believe me. We stepped onto the street as horse hooves clip-clopped closer. Mohsin, the horseman who came by our house each morning to take us riding, ambled by with three horses behind him. I asked him if he had ever seen anyone living in the double-storied house.

Mohsin was not in a hurry. He deposited himself on a stone chalked with white paint to mark the edge of the street and stroked his white beard. "Bibi, an Angrez British Sahib lived here before Partition, many years ago. Poor man. He had a beautiful daughter. Every Englishman was wanting to marry her. But she chose a Pakistani doctor. They had a son. One evening, her husband went to buy paint for his son—he was also a craftsman and made toys for children. This time was special—he was making a present for his boy. One train set."

I nudged Shireen's ribs.

"The doctor got caught in a storm. He fell into a ravine. Broke his neck. His wife and son were left with her father. Broken-hearted, Memsahib decided to leave Hawagali. She packed a few belongings. With her son, she stepped into a horse carriage to return to Murree where the doctor's family lived. A storm started up. Their driver took a wrong turn, and their carriage overturned. Mother and son died instantly. Memsahib's father packed his things and left Hawagali forever. No one knows if he returned to England, or if he hid in the mountains until he, too, passed away."

"When did these incidents take place?" I asked, my words tripping over each other.

Mohsin scratched his bald head and his wrinkles deepened. "Perhaps fifty years ago." He got up from the white stone. "I remember. I was a little boy. Village people say that Memsahib roams the mountainside looking for her husband. Sometimes they see her with her son. Other times she's alone. Poor lady." Shaking his head, Mohsin sauntered off with his horses.

I put my hand over my mouth as his figure receded. "Shireen, I think I had tea with a kaneez!" I whispered.

Shireen couldn't find words to respond to me.

*　　*　　*

Sameer and Saira sit up on their knees. "Nani, you can't stop there!" Sameer shouts. "You're saying that Alice was a witch—or a ghost?"

"Unless you have a better answer."

"You never found anything more?"

I pick cat hairs off the sofa. "No. But, that's how the mountains are: full of mystery. The light, sounds, and foliage contribute to the magic. One day, perhaps we can go north together. I can also search for the train carriage to show you."

Behind her glasses, Saira's eyebrows are knit. "Does Mom know this story?"

I nod.

"Her brother died there, didn't he?"

"Yes."

"What happened to him?" Saira's voice is low.

My hand is at my throat. "He got caught in a storm. His accident had nothing to do with these stories. It's time for bed."

Without protest, Saira and Sameer slip out of the room, arms linked, walking closer than I have seen them.

They will ask many more questions.

six

YASMEEN

Carlos' skin, dark against his gleaming teeth and white T-shirt, was swarthier in the unlit corridor. The night-guard nodded and receded down the hallway, his footsteps sounding like basketballs on the wooden floor.

"May I come in Profesora?" Carlos asked. He called me Profesora when I was at work, saying that I looked academic when I wore my reading glasses.

I slipped behind my desk. "When did you get back?"

"A few days ago. Hope you don't mind that I dropped by?" He settled in my visitor's chair. "I was passing by and saw your car. I begged the guard to show me in. Am I catching you at a bad time?"

I glanced at my coffee mug. "It's been a shitty day, and I'm working on a deadline…"

"And now I'm here?" Carlos finished. Leaning forward, he watched me restack papers.

I took off my reading glasses. "I just have a lot going on."

He stood up and wiped his hands on his jeans. "I'm sorry. I should've called. This is about Phoenix, isn't it?"

"Please sit, Carlos." I didn't want him to leave. "You're right, we do need to talk."

"We were away, and now we're here. What's the problem?"

Ignoring the no-smoking rule in my office, I lit up. "I'm sorry. Things are crazy. My mother's in town." I exhaled. "I don't have room for complications."

"We were in a new place and got carried away. So what? We're adults. And that wasn't our first time together. Though our exchange was steamier than I remember." He grinned. When I didn't return his smile, he wiped his hand over his mouth as if to clear his face. "What happened was circumstantial. I'm happy to carry on as before. Go running at Memorial, meet at happy hours, take your kids to the movies. Whatever."

I ran my hands through my hair. When Jim and I decided to divorce, we hired lawyers. By the time he and I signed papers, we no longer understood why we had chosen to be with each other. Cutting away one decade of my life felt as if I had amputated a leg and had to learn how to walk without limping. And Jim and I still had to share our children. I needed time for the experience to fade before I could walk without a crutch. "Circumstantial?"

Carlos leaned forward, resting his chin on his palms lying flat on the desk. "Yes, you know, red earth, wild animals, primordial desire, and all that..."

I glanced above Carlos' curly hair, aware that the attraction that I felt toward him was matched by an equally strong desire to run while I could. The electricity was as tangible as a wire that stretched from his hands to mine.

"In Arizona, I was floating...out of control," I said. "But when I returned to Houston, I had to deal with reality. Phoenix was too much of an escape." I lit another cigarette.

"I understand. I felt out of control myself. I came by, you know, to talk. I wanted to see how you are. Haven't seen you in months, no email, nothing. Just thought I'd check in."

From behind smoke spirals, I studied Carlos' steady brown eyes, his smooth forehead, and his closed smile that reminded me of a purring cat.

"So screw Arizona. We can still be friends."

I laughed in spite of myself. Carlos had a way of disarming me. "We're not in kindergarten. Of course, you're my friend."

Carlos' chuckle bounced around my office walls. "There's no problem then."

I thought about afternoons when he and I had shared sandwiches at the Menil Collection's park, or times that he had joined me to watch Saira play soccer or Sam play baseball. Long before the divorce, without my saying anything, Carlos had known that my marriage was over, but he never pushed me to do anything more. And he was the person that I had called when Saira was harassed at school. "You're right, there isn't a problem." Saying the words out loud was a revelation to me. "I'm still adjusting to my new life and today's reality. Being a single mother, in a formal manner, is different. I've missed you as a friend. Let's let things be for now."

Carlos threw his head back and laughed. "Sounds good to me." His smile faded. "Next time you want to run, slow down and talk."

I reached out and touched his palm. "I'm sorry. I'm glad you stopped by."

"Okay, now here's the big question: what the hell are you doing at work on a Friday night?"

"A crazy report for Henrietta."

"Aah, Henrietta. Slavedriver." He reached over for my pack of cigarettes and took a drag before coughing. "I can't smoke!! Let's get out of here."

I reached for my jacket. I deserved time off.

Still grinning, Carlos looked over his shoulder. "Don't let Slavedriver know it was my fault that you left early. She already thinks I'm a degenerate!"

Henrietta had met Carlos at several office parties. When left alone with him, her eyes darted around the room like marbles rolling, searching for an exit. Carlos, knowing she wanted to hobnob with executives, relished prolonging her discomfort by exaggerating stories about his travels.

I would call Henrietta in the morning and tell her that my computer had crashed. Or perhaps, for once, I would tell her the truth: I did have a life.

*   *   *

In Carlos' kitchen, I whisked eggs, while he heated the pan and took tortillas out of the refrigerator. "I'm sorry for being grumpy in the office. But you always show up at the right time."

"Built-in radar."

Perhaps his intuition came from being an only child and an orphan. Long ago, he told me about how his father had swept his mother off her feet. "They married a week after they met. My dad brought home fresh bread and flowers every week." Carlos' expression darkened as he told me about his parents' car accident. Twelve at the time, Carlos was adopted by his father's sister, Maria. His parents' romantic marriage was so different from Amman's and Abu's arranged one, making his parents' accident all the more tragic.

For dessert, he heated hot chocolate that his aunt Maria had sent to him. "She prepares this hot chocolate for us each new year's day."

I closed my eyes and savored the flavor. "I'll pretend we're on holiday."

"I wish. But vacation is around the corner!" He clinked his mug against mine. "Here's to the upcoming year. May it be better. Shit, anything's got to be better than this one."

"Yes, the year from hell. At least you were away in September. Our reality changed, and I don't see how we can revert to life before 9/11." My cheeks felt hot as tears welled. The only times I remembered crying with another person was when I talked to Yasir, who comforted me and made me laugh so hard that I forgot the reason I wept. I wiped my eyes with my sleeve. "Of course, I've complicated life further by having my mother here. Jim was gone, I wanted change—so I invited her. But I didn't realize that her presence would evoke so many memories. I should have known. After all, I had cut off from her for a reason. I didn't want to remember.

"Last night I dreamed that my twin and I were wearing a blue sweater that my mother had knitted for us. We were warm and had to unravel the wool in order to take the sweater off. But the string was infinite. The more wool we pulled, the more sweater there was. I woke up crying. I needed him to tell me how the dream ended. But he wasn't there. I wake up every day with dreams that don't have endings. Sounds crazy doesn't it?"

Carlos unpeeled a pine nut and popped it in his mouth. "No. I just can't even imagine how it feels to have a twin with whom you share so much..."

"Everything's being kicked up for me because my mother's telling the kids stories about our mountain home. That's where he...died."

"Maybe she gets peace by sharing stories?" Carlos prodded a log, causing the fire to hiss. "I was young when my parents died, and I wouldn't know anything about them if Tía María and other family members hadn't told me about them. I like knowing that my father hated to cook, but he still made the best chicken soup in all of San

Francisco. My people have a celebration to remember those who have passed on. Similar rituals exist in all cultures. We shouldn't forget those who have passed on. I've known you for a long time, but this is the first time that you've talked about your family…"

"When I tell stories about Yasir, I cry." I dabbed my eyes with a tissue. "Amman's being here makes life different. And there's already change around us…"

"I'm glad I was out of the country when the towers collapsed. Returning to Houston was surreal. The airport was crowded with guards holding guns. Security opened and examined every piece of my luggage."

The gaps in my own life had become more stark since the World Trade Center explosions. Though I had not experienced danger myself, friends told me about men wearing turbans—who weren't even Muslim—being attacked and killed in New York, parts of Houston, and around the country. If I expressed anger at the backlash, friends told me to "be careful" and that "now's not the time to criticize the government." Certainly, the incident at Saira's school should have been handled differently.

Feeling like a helium balloon, I floated without a string. Perhaps I had invited Amman to Houston with the hope that her presence might ground me and help me find peace.

*   *   *

I entered the house through the kitchen door. The kitchen was dark, but I knew my way to the refrigerator. As I opened the refrigerator, someone turned on the kitchen light.

Amman stood behind me holding a broomstick like a sword. "I was worried. I thought I heard a dacoit."

Using paper towels, I dried the water that I spilled. "Dacoit? Robbers? Please don't worry so much! We have an alarm system—we're safe."

Amman set the broom down. "I'm sorry."

"Amman, I'm thirty-six. Mother of two. I do stay out late sometimes. I'll let you know next time, so please don't worry."

She nodded. "Thank you. You'll always be my child. Baita, you work too hard. If I weren't here, who would look after the children?"

I leaned against the sink. "I appreciate your help. I really do…"

I wanted to tell her how much I had cried before sending her the invitation, but the words wouldn't leave my mouth.

"I enjoy every minute with the children." She paused. "But they also need you around."

Turning off the light, I slipped past her, whispering, "Goodnight."

seven

YASMEEN

The after-dinner scene was familiar: Saira reading a book in front of the fire; Sam on his stomach with his face propped up by his palms, watching television; and me in my sweatpants, reading the newspaper on the sofa. Amman was in Brenham.

Saira looked up from her book, caught my eye, and flashed me a smile. Her moods seemed to have stabilized since the boys had stopped teasing her, but she was still isolating herself. According to her teacher, Saira buried her nose in a book during recess. At her last eye doctor visit, we learned that her eyesight had deteriorated further. My vacation was around the corner, and I looked forward to spending time with the children.

"Why did Nani have to visit relatives?" Sam's question pulled me away from my study of Saira.

"Because she hadn't seen them in a while."

"Who're they?" Saira asked without looking up. "Are they our family, too?"

"Good question. Yes, Safia is my second cousin, the daughter of your Nani's first cousin."

"How come you never tell us stories, Mom?" asked Sam, losing interest in family. His lip jutted out, looking as if it would curl over and meet his chin.

Saira's glasses slipped down her nose. "There's no point asking her."

I wished we didn't have to wait for another week for my vacation to start. The semester was so hectic with soccer and baseball practice, playdates, and after-school activities. We never had time to relax. I expelled a deep breath. "You need to go to bed. School's tomorrow, remember? I'll give you five minutes." I returned to my unread morning paper.

An object thudded against the wall behind me. Sam's sneaker had landed on the other end of the room. The shoe lay still, black sole facing the ceiling.

"Pick that up! It's bad luck to leave shoes facing god." The children's expressions forced me to think about my words: I had expressed a superstition—one that I didn't even believe—that my Dadi had drummed in my consciousness. "I mean—pick up that shoe! Your behavior's unacceptable."

Sam's hair shaded his eyes as he slithered toward the shoe. His lips trembled. "I wanna go to Dad's."

My breath caught at the base of my throat. I joined him on the floor, but he shied away. "I'm sorry, little one." I covered his long fingers—just like Yasir's—with my palms. "Tell you what, you two get ready for bed. I'll come up and tell you a story—from when I was little. Like your Nani does."

Saira looked up, her face blank. As my comment registered, she leapt up and scampered up the stairs. Sam followed behind her. A minute later, I heard them fighting over the bathroom sink. I shook my head. I didn't know that stories from home would grip them. Picking up glasses, I dusted cookie crumbs off the sofa.

I picked up Sam's overturned shoe and placed it on the shoe stand. My grandmother never used to touch slippers with her fingers. She wore them on her feet, but if she ever so much as brushed the bottom of the shoes with her hand, she squatted by her sink for hours trying to re-purify her skin. A quirky woman. I knew that Dadi and Amman had been close before Abu passed away, and she had supported Amman whenever my father exploded. Dealing with my own kids, I could begin to understand the challenges that Yasir and I had presented our Dadi.

I switched off the television, clamping down on my impulse to bolt out of the house, leap into my car, and drive into the night. Dadi hated noise. Each week, she used to yell at Doodwallah—the milkman who supplied our house with fresh milk—for blowing his scooter horn and talking in a loud voice.

"Mom, we're in bed," Saira called.

In their dark room, I tucked the children's comforters close to their faces and sat on the rocking chair.

"You're going to tell us about witches, yeah?" Sam asked.

"Not today."

"Is your brother in this story?" Saira's voice was low. They had seen photos of Yasir, and I had told them a little about him. Since Amman had shared a few stories about her childhood, Saira and Sam wanted to learn more about the uncle they had never met.

I expelled a breath.

*   *   *

In 1971 when Yasir and I were a little younger than you and Sam are today, your Nani and my father had flown to London for some business. So my twin and I moved upstairs to stay with our grandparents, Dadi and Dada. We didn't know that our army had begun violence in East Pakistan to clamp down on the Bengali independence movement that had escalated.

But one December morning, West Pakistan was directly impacted by the war when the Indian government got involved and began maneuvering airstrikes. We were at our breakfast table when the Mullah—the priest from our street mosque—cleared his throat over the loudspeakers that were fastened on the mosque minarets.

"Attention! Attention!" he rasped over loudspeakers that he used to announce prayer times. "Government orders! All people must cover house windows!"

"Why do they want our windows covered?" Yasir asked Dada.

Dada lowered the volume of his radio and frowned. "For blackout," he said. "So the Indian army will not know where to bomb."

Outside, the Mullah's voice, like a prerecorded announcement, droned on showing little sign of stopping. Once the din from the mosque ended, we sat in the car as Dada and our driver headed to the market to purchase supplies. Our street bustled as people stuffed straw baskets with ropes, candles, tinned food, batteries, and torches.

By mid-afternoon, our electrician Aftab Chacha had plugged in the hot plate and the radio. Our windows were covered with newspaper, and our house was war-ready. Dada emerged from his room to give his verdict on the windows. When the telephone jangled, everyone froze to stare at the black instrument as if soldiers were about to charge out of the receiver. Dada strode over and picked up the handle. Our family friend Dr. Javed was on the phone, inviting us to join him on the other side of town at the 'bomb shelter' that he had devised in his basement.

"No sir," Dada responded. "We will have a top class view of airplanes from our own balcony. The children will be fine here with us, indeed." He hung up laughing, but I could tell he was nervous by the way he chewed his lip.

After sunset, we heard a new sound, this time from a van that circled our neighborhood, sounding the blackout signal. The eerie noise devoured the stillness, giving us the signal to turn off all lights. The siren also meant that curfew had begun and that people could no longer leave their houses.

Yasir and I wandered to the kitchen to chat with Aftab Chacha and our driver, Jamshed. Both men, unlike other grownups, were not interested in monitoring war events: Aftab Chacha didn't like to talk about events that made him sad—his entire family had died of small-pox and he still had pock-marks on his face, while twenty-three year-old Jamshed, played cricket with us as if he were a ten-year-old.

Aftab Chacha, one of the few members of hired help who could read, squatted on a floor stool and pulled out an Urdu newspaper. Pointing his torch on a blurry picture of upside-down acrobats in sequined costumes, he said. "See here, it says a circus will be in Karachi next week. That's three days away." He switched off the torch.

Jamshed spoke first. "Can we go, Aftab Bhai?"

Aftab Chacha nodded. "If we don't get killed by a bomb before..."

A thought occurred to me. "How's there a circus if we're at war?"

Aftab Chacha puffed his cigarette. "They were planning the circus before the war was declared. I'm sure they'll end the acts early, so people can get to their houses before blackout time." His belly wobbled between the waistband of his pants and his shirt. "These are dangerous times."

"Can we go?" my twin asked.

"Your Dadi won't permit you to go with us," Aftab Chacha replied. Yasir and I grumbled under our breaths. Our life in Karachi was different from your experience in Houston. There, we could not wander outside the walls that protected our home. We drove everywhere—to homes, school, and the club where we learned to swim and play tennis."

Late that night, we heard bombs exploding. From afar, we watched as oil refineries lit up in flames, burning holes in the dark horizon while shells exploded in the sky like fireworks. The roar of airplanes kept us up that night. We stayed awake holding each other's hands. Even when I finally fell asleep, I had dreams about maps burning at the borders where mothers held their dying children. But when morning came, no one talked to us and told us what was happening. Even the newspaper did not have real news.

"Everything will be fine," my Dada said without meeting my eyes.

Yasir and I had forgotten about the circus until Aftab Chacha and Jamshed had already gone. They sat in the kitchen and couldn't stop talking about the sights they had seen. Yasir and I came up with our own plan when we overheard them talking about how they would see the circus' last Karachi show, which was ending a week early because of the war.

The following afternoon, Aftab Chacha entered through our back gate and disappeared into Jamshed's quarter. Yasir and I were on the lookout. As they stepped out, we jumped up from behind the courtyard's low wall.

"Surprise!" we shouted.

Aftab Chacha and Jamshed were ready to drop their plans, but we promised to buy their tickets from money in our piggy bank. They agreed to take us, knowing that Dadi and Dada were napping and that we wouldn't be missed since we would return by teatime, well before blackout.

*　　*　　*

I stopped.

The children squealed in unison for the first time that evening: "Mom—what happened next?"

I was amazed at the unraveling of the story from a place so deep within me that I had forgotten that the narrative even existed. The final ten days of war on our side of the border were deeply embedded in me: Our war-ready house, the air-raid siren plummeting the city in a blackout; the swishing of curfew vans followed by a dead calm that was ripped apart when airplanes roared in the sky. These were sights and sounds that had lived inside me for more than three decades.

Much later, we learned about the atrocities that the Pakistani army had committed in Bangladesh.

Now, living at a time of violence, I was not surprised that the first story that I told my children was about war. I pondered whether I should even be sharing such tales with Saira and Sam. But on the other hand, I had to show them—and perhaps even myself—that one had to push past darkness to find magic when the world around us spun like a spindle without a thread.

*   *   *

The four of us slipped out of the back gate, hopped on a bus, and reached the corner where the circus was being held. But the sight that greeted us was not the distraction that we expected. The tent was a rectangular enclosure made of shamiyanas—colorful cloth partitions that people used for weddings—and not the big-top circle we expected. We saw a few monkeys in a cage, a horse tied to a pole, and a mule chewing on brown grass, while performers strolled, sucking on cigarettes. Men sat on benches, smoking cigarettes, and there were no caravans or wild animals. Jamshed and Aftab Chacha pulled us to the man who sold the tickets at half-price.

The circus began late, but the afternoon light revealed dingy costumes, dirty seats, and seedy men laughing at card tricks and dagger shots that even I knew were not magical. At our birthday parties, we had better snake and puppet shows.

After the circus ended, we headed home. Yasir and I had little to say, but Aftab Chacha and Jamshed couldn't stop raving about the magician's skills. Yasir and I walked fast, hoping that we could get a taxi and be home before we were missed. To get found out and be punished for the anticlimactic escapade would be terrible.

Aftab Chacha and Jamshed fell silent as they tried to flag a rickshaw, a taxi, a horse carriage—anything to take us home—but the streets had cleared and the sun was dropping low. We stumbled over cracks in the sidewalk, and our sandals soon filled with dirt. Darkness fell like a blanket covering not only buildings, but also all the people and cars in our world.

We finally reached the intersection where our street met the main road. All we had to do was walk down the narrow street and we would be home. Just then, a hollow trumpet sound arose as if it were swelling from beneath the earth, making my lungs feel like an inflated mattress. The black-out siren was earlier than usual, signaling an air-raid. Vans sending the signal crisscrossed the streets, and the siren faded and grew, faded and grew. When silence fell, I felt my breath ebb away.

A new sound erupted: approaching enemy airplanes. A blast echoed. With our hands clasped over our heads as if that would protect us from shells, we ran through the potholed street. The sky exploded in a burst of flames. I stopped running to crouch next to a small shack's tin door. Another bomb exploded above us. I pushed against the door, and I fell inside a room with dirt floors.

In front of me stood a red-bearded man, the milkman whom we called Doodwallah. His expression mirrored my surprise. He motioned the rest of us inside the lantern-lit room where a petite woman bent over a stove, her back towards us, making tea. Two children sat on a charpoy-bed, their mouths agape. Shelves hammered into the walls held plates, spices, and other kitchenware.

I remembered Dadi scolding Doodwallah about his loud voice. She might not approve of us being in his room. "So loud!" I could see her saying with a sniff of her nose.

Through all those years of Doodwallah delivering milk, Yasir and I had never realized that he lived close-by and that his living space would be so different from ours. We had an upstairs and downstairs with bedrooms, living rooms, windows, hallways, and separate kitchens. Here, the Doodwallah, his wife, and their children seemed to cook, eat, and sleep in the same space.

Doodwallah shook his head and invited us to make ourselves comfortable. "Things are very bad in this world," he said, shaking his head.

Even though we were in as much danger inside as we were outside, we found comfort to be off the streets where shells exploded and fires flared.

Doodwallah and his wife offered us milk and naan. In the lantern light, Doodwallah reached over to Yasir and drew out a 25-paisa coin from behind Yasir's ear. "Why do you hide money, Baba?" he asked.

Our eyes widened.

"You like magic? I can make coins appear and disappear." He replaced the coin behind Yasir's ear, but when Yasir reached for the coin, it was no longer there. Doodwallah waved his hands, reached behind Yasir's other ear and pulled out the coin. We clapped our hands.

Doodwallah asked his wife for an egg, which he broke into a bowl. Waving his hands, he lifted the egg from beneath a cloth, and drew it out intact, no crack showing. From outside, we could hear the rattle of airplanes and explosions, but in Doodwallah's room, we forgot about bombings. Even Jamshed and Aftab Chacha agreed that Doodwallah was better than the circus magician.

At around eight in the evening, there was a lull in the bombings. We used the opportunity to bid our hosts goodnight and slip into the street.

"Give my respects to your Dadi," Doodwallah's voice boomed. We felt as if we were emerging from a dream in which the Doodwallah's magic protected us from fire in a distant corner of our city.

*   *   *

"And that's how we saw magic during wartime," I ended.

Sam sat up. "You never got in trouble for going out without permission?"

I shook my head. "We told our grandparents that we were in a shop when the bombing started and had to take shelter. They were relieved that we were safe—they had been worried about us."

Saira spoke up. "What about the war?"

I stood up. "The war with India ended two days later. Pakistan was defeated and Bangladesh gained independence. Doodwallah was a wise man. Till today, I remember his words. I was only six or seven at the time, but I can't forget what he said. 'These are the wars of big men. The voices of milkmen, electricians, drivers don't matter. These men will fight and kill our brothers no matter what. The Bengalis want freedom. They are not our enemies.'"

Sam opened his eyes a crack. "Mom, do you miss your brother?"

I held my breath and then released it slowly. "Very much."

Saira snuggled closer to her pillow. "It's good you have us."

"Yes, it is. Go to sleep now."

Saira sat up. "My gym teacher said that some bad guys will do more explosions in America... Is that true, Mom?"

I made a mental note to talk to the teacher and find out why he was spreading media hype amidst the kids. "That's not true. Even if we experience war, I'll be with you." I dropped kisses on their foreheads, tightened their comforters, and remained in the rocking chair till they fell asleep.

Talking to the children about Karachi and about my twin for the first time made me feel as if a vessel in my lungs had opened, and I was breathing again. The world in which I had grown up was different from the life I lived in the US. For many years, I had gone to work, spent Halloween and Christmas with the kids, but I had not told them about my experiences when I was their age: rising at dawn to eat greasy parathas and then fasting all day, shopping for glass bangles after the new moon sighting, and dressing up for Eid to receive crisp rupee notes from elders. After Yasir's passing and my departure from Karachi, all I wanted to do was to forget. But I wasn't so sure about anything anymore.

At work, I knew that I was different from the people I worked with. I didn't drape flags around my car, nor did I follow Fox headlines. In that moment, I realized that I wanted to give the children a glimpse of a world, I wanted them to understand histories beyond what they knew in Houston and what they were taught in school.

In my room, I lay on my bed and cried as though my heart had been splintered open like the bombs that had ripped through the Karachi sky. I cried for the devastation in East Pakistan, for the history that I was never taught.

I wept for plans that Yasir and I made to build a boat and travel around the world and meet twins in Bangladesh, Indonesia, New Zealand, Iceland, Guam, Mauritius. In our boat, twins of the world would gather and spin stories together. I cried, knowing that all I wanted was to go to sleep, and for Yasir to wake me up so we could share the beginnings and endings of our dreams after which we could clamber up to the roof and fly kites together.

eight

LAILA

I fill the kettle with water and turn the knob. A yellow flame, blue at its base, shoots to life. My Karachi stove never lights without matches. One more week and I will leave. Pausing to gulp hot tea, I click my knitting needles, determined to complete Yasmeen's sweater before I fly home. In Karachi, I don't care for sugar in my tea, but here, I need extra energy.

The view from the window is quiet. In Yasmeen's neighborhood, one never sees people, except for faces flitting behind tinted windows of passing cars. Sometimes, I hear a neighbor's garage door roll open. A car pulls out, and the garage door folds as the car drives away on the empty road. The grounds of our Clifton house are quiet because we are sealed off from the street by six feet high cement walls, atop of which are chipped glass to prevent robbers from breaking in. But outside the gate, a stream of pedestrians—dhobis-laundrymen, bus boys, cleaning women, beggars, men with food carts—stop beneath the gulmohr tree to drink water from the pitcher that we leave outside and to talk with our chowkidar-watchman.

Yasmeen's house is silent, breathing with a life of its own. The children are with their father while Yasmeen is at work. I would not want to live in this space, each room feeling as if it contains clouds of bitter turmeric even though Yasmeen never cooks with Pakistani spices. A few days ago Yasmeen told me she wants to move to a new house.

Uneasy in a space filled with sad memories, I say, "Good idea."

*   *   *

Yasmeen remains outside most of the day tending to weeds in her garden with headphones wrapped around her head. During lunch, she reminds me of a new year's eve party to which we are invited.

"My friends want to meet you," she says. "The drive is far, but the gathering will be fun."

Nodding my assent, I put my knitting down. A drive together might be what we need so we can talk.

As soon as she exits her neighborhood and enters the freeway, I gaze out of the window and speak. "Baita, I wasn't the best mother to you all the time. Perhaps you can talk to me and let me support you in your life today? Everyone at home waits for news about you. They want to see you and meet the children."

Yasmeen's eyes remain pinned on the road.

"Fazila asks about you all the time. She wants to visit you."

Yasmeen curves the car around a truck that has a cylindrical tank attached to its back. "Baita, is America your true home now?"

She shakes her head. "I don't know."

"Then why don't you return to Karachi for a visit? You need to do that so you can settle your heart."

"We will—one day."

"Don't wait too long, Baita. Time moves fast. Your father is no longer with us. Neither are your grandparents. Many others will pass away. Set aside your pain. Move forward, Baita. Come and visit."

Yasmeen nods. "We can talk more later. I need to concentrate on driving." She reaches forward and turns up the radio. The discussion is over.

*   *   *

Yasmeen's friend Janet greets us with a smile, holding out her arms to me as if she knows me. "I'm so happy to meet you," she says. "I've heard a lot about you." The fragrance of fresh basil and red pepper emanates from the kitchen. "I'm cooking something different today," Janet says. "I learned it in a cooking class."

Yasmeen's face lights up. She extends her smile to me and says, "Janet likes to treat us like her guinea pigs." She nudges Janet's ribs.

"What're you experimenting with this time?"

Janet laughs. "Thai food. You may get lucky if you let me finish."

Yasmeen ushers Janet into the kitchen and leads me to the living room where she introduces me to Janet's husband, Tony, who sits in a corner, his fingers sliding over a guitar. He's a musician, Yasmeen informs me.

A shorter man with dark curly hair leans against the fireplace. Seeing us enter, he straightens and approaches us.

"Amman, this is Carlos," Yasmeen's cheeks are flushed as if the room has warmed up.

Carlos kisses Yasmeen on both cheeks and shakes my hand. Yasmeen, regal in a purple dress with long sleeves, is at home in this house where Tony jokes with her as if she were his sister. She wanders into the kitchen to help her friend while Tony and his sons step outside to play basketball in the driveway, leaving Carlos and me in the drawing room. I examine framed photographs.

From behind me, Carlos says. "Those are Janet's sisters."

I turn around. "She's from a large family?"

"One of ten children. That's her mom." He points to an image of a round-faced woman wearing a pearl necklace and a black collared blouse. "You'd never believe it to look at her, would you?"

"She does look young. And you? How many sisters and brothers do you have?"

"Just me."

"That must have been difficult?"

His teeth are a shot of white gleam. "Not really. I had cousins and friends." From the driveway, Tony's shouts float into the room, and Carlos changes the subject. "I've seen Yasmeen's paintings. She does these beautiful scenes from Pakistan. I've always been interested in your part of the world—long before the Al-Qaeda round-up began. Now with the US invasion of Afghanistan, South Asia is always in the news."

"The first time I visited this country—while Yasmeen was in college—people didn't even know where Pakistan was."

"I'm a historian, and I've studied your region's history." He pauses. "So, is your President-General Musharraf going to survive? The press here thinks that extremists will dislodge him soon."

"Sometimes news reports are sensational. The religious extremists are only five percent of our population. But of course, when CNN covers news about Pakistan, they look for mullahs and women in hijab."

Carlos shakes his head. "True. Yasmeen's told me a lot about your family's mountain house. Is it safe to go there?"

I raise my eyebrows. "That side of the mountains is away from Afghanistan border and India, so we don't experience much trouble there. The conflict in Pakistan is decades old—started in the late 1970's when the Russians invaded Afghanistan and the US government poured weapons into Pakistan. But the hill country area has remained conflict-free."

I find myself talking to Yasmeen's friend as if I have known him from another time. Or perhaps he is a good listener. "My father bought the summer home before I was even born when the British Raj was still in India. Over the years, the hill stations became fashionable. Prices rose and new construction started. But each summer, I took Yasmeen and her twin to our mountain home."

I adjust my sari and watch Tony chase after his son. The thump of the orange basketball reverberates through glass windows that are without burglar bars—unlike Pakistani homes where windows are protected by steel grills. Yasir was not much of a sports fan, but he was more alive and active whenever we were in Hawagali.

"My son—before he passed away—he spent too much time relaxing, smoking, listening to music. He wasn't living up to his potential at school. His father used to threaten him that he wouldn't be able to travel in the summer unless his report card improved. That made my son angry because the children loved their time in the mountains."

Carlos nods. "My Dad used to push me to study more. He was good at emotionally blackmailing me."

I watch Tony and his son bounce the orange ball. "Just before his...accident, Yasir had a fight with his father. You see, my son was an artist. He didn't want to study business, but that's what his father wanted for him. Yasir was his only son, and my husband felt that someone had to take over the family business. And then... and then, the accident happened. I haven't returned to Hawagali since. Nothing's been the same since his passing. And Yasmeen, she left the country. She never recovered from losing her twin. No one has..."

Carlos nods. "I'm sorry."

"Yasmeen tells me that you lost your parents. That must be difficult to bear. For me, just hearing my son's name makes my eyes tear up... I keep him alive by telling stories about him. And Yasmeen doesn't understand that. How do you heal if you don't grieve, if you don't tell stories? Her life is shattered. I feel hopeful when I see what good friends she has, but I worry about my daughter. How can she find peace when she's so far from her home, cut off from people who love her?"

Carlos doesn't answer. Yasmeen has entered the room to set the table. I don't know how much she overheard.

"Dinner will be served in a minute!" she says.

When we sit down to eat, Yasmeen places herself on the opposite side of the table from me and barely touches the red curry and noodles. Once the table is cleared, she picks up her purse.

Tony looks up from filling the dishwasher: "We still need to play Pictionary!"

"Who will draw if you leave?" Carlos throws in.

Her back unbending, Yasmeen hugs her friends one by one, and they walk us to the car. Pulling out of the driveway onto the road in one motion, Yasmeen drives past houses lit up with string lights. One hand grips the wheel while she changes gears with the other. I strap on my safety belt and clutch the handlebar to my side. We pass a street where a family unloads from a car. Yasmeen swings around a corner. Her tires peal as her headlights beam on the children's faces.

"Baita, maybe you should slow down," I say.

She accelerates. A green light turns yellow and is red by the time we pass. The driver on the other side sounds his horn.

Once Yasmeen pulls into her garage, she steps into the house without waiting for me. Behind me, the garage door rumbles and closes. I unsnap the car handle, wondering why my daughter has a compulsion to lock doors. I wouldn't be surprised if I have to knock to be allowed inside.

nine

LAILA

The kitchen is dark except for the slat of light that emits from the open refrigerator door. "I enjoyed meeting your friends," I say.

Without turning around, Yasmeen takes a gulp of water.

"They're nice. Janet is very beautiful."

"Yes."

I sit down at the kitchen table. "Can you talk about why you're so upset?"

Yasmeen closes the fridge door.

I blink my eyes to adjust to the darkness. "Many years have slipped away since you have talked to me. Why stay silent? ... Don't bottle up your anger."

She turns away. "You should know..."

I stand up. I'm reaching my limit with my daughter. She talks even less than she did when she was a young girl. At least back then she had a twin who told me things that I needed to know. Yasmeen never articulated why she stopped phoning me, or why she stopped sending me letters.

Yasmeen slams her glass on the kitchen table. Water sloshes over the rim. "I just want you to leave things alone. You don't need to discuss me with my friends. The accident happened. He's gone. Nothing can bring him back..."

I hold back my tears. "I understand your pain, Baita. Yasir was my son."

"Yasir." She says his name as if she has tossed a stone into a black pond, a stone that drops into the depths of the water, causing no ripples.

"We have to remember him by celebrating his life." The words belong to my older sister, but I repeat the line often so I can believe it to be true. "He had a good life. We have to celebrate the joys that we shared."

Yasmeen flicks the light switch. Her action makes me blink.

"I'm ready to let the past go. You're the one stuck there. That's why I don't talk about what happened in Hawagali."

"Baita, don't fight me. How long will you run from yourself?"

"What do you mean?" Her voice is soft.

"We let you fly halfway around the world, but we didn't know you would not return. How much longer will you stay away?"

"I'm trying to make a life for myself after you wrecked it."

I take a deep breath.

"Yasir's accident—it was your fault."

Anger licks my throat.

"I invited you in a moment of impulse. I felt sorry for you, alone in Karachi."

She says nothing about how lonely she must have felt after her divorce. Her letter reached me just a few months after the paperwork was formalized. I knew my daughter's handwriting; after all, I was the one who taught her how to write her name and her brother's name in Urdu and in English.

I watch her grope in her purse and draw out a cigarette.

"We have to accept our loss," I say. "Blaming others won't bring him back."

She stops pacing. "He went out that night to look for you. You said you were with Heera. But you weren't with her. She can't walk fast. Or far."

Behind my closed eyelids I see the image of my son, stumbling through rain and boulders.

Yasmeen continues, her voice low. "Thunder was rolling that night. Remember?"

"Yes. I remember."

"I saw lightning crackle when you came to see me. You were dressed up—earrings and a fancy kurta in the mountains!" Her voice is sarcastic.

My hands tremble as I tuck a strand of hair behind my ear.

"You and Abu had a fight that night. I remember him shouting. What were you fighting about?"

"You've been through a divorce. People argue."

Yasmeen's shoulders drop. "You want me to believe that you and Abu had a normal marriage?"

"I'll talk to you once you calm down." She has a right to ask questions, but not when she spits two decades of pain upon me. I, too, have sorrow, but I have no one to blame.

"Who were you with when the storm hit? You weren't outside?" Yasmeen's chin is an accusing finger.

I stumble to the door.

Her voice drops. "I was sick. But I remember your perfume. And the song you hummed."

"Baita, I have relived that night a thousand times. I wasn't much older than you are today. I would give up my life to bring Yasir back." Tears shroud my eyes. I walk away from the kitchen to my bedroom and close the door.

Memories crowd my mind: Tariq's thundering voice, Yasmeen's forehead burning with fever, Heera's firm hands, holding mine, begging me to calm myself. His smooth chest, my Qais. I cover my face with the blanket just as I had done with a chaddar during my illicit visits. I could not open the doorway to enter those years. My shoulders shake. Yasmeen's accusations are earthquakes that shake my foundation, rocking the stability that I have built brick by brick since the accident.

*   *   *

A month prior to my wedding, after my family refuses *his* marriage proposal to me, I lock myself in my room, crying, begging them to call off my engagement to Tariq. My mother sends Sikandar to me, knowing that I cannot refuse my eldest brother.

"They are our parents," Sikandar says. "They want the best for you. Tariq is a good man. Well respected. He doesn't want a dowry. He wants to help our family business. Think of your izzat, the family's izzat. Everyone's honor is at stake here."

I stare at my hennaed hands, red in preparation for the wedding. I know that my father will go bankrupt if he doesn't receive money from somewhere. "You want me to give up my life so you can have yours?"

My mother enters the room to sit on the bed beside me. She takes off her chappals and puts her scuffed toes on top of each other. "Your Abba came from India, sold clothes and shoes to the English," she says. "He built the factory before they left. But the Angrez are gone. If things continue the way they are, I don't know what will happen. We'll have to sell everything—including our home in Hawagali. If you marry Tariq, he'll invest in your father's business." Her thin cheeks are creased from days of weeping.

In that moment I press my lips together. With my eyes pinned on my mother's face hidden behind her knobby hands, I make the decision to marry Tariq.

On my wedding night, I sit on a stage, my head covered by an embroidered dupatta, bowed by jewelry from Tariq's family, aware of my husband's breath, and the fragrance of his rose petal garland. Tariq's gold rings remind me of how his wealth saved our family. After the wedding, we fly with my five suitcases to Karachi where I weep each day. But Tariq does what he promised: he invests in my family's 'Pindi business and the crisis is averted.

To me, Tariq shows more patience than I dreamed he would, passing no comments when, each evening after he returns from work, he finds me seated by the telephone, my eyes red. "Bridal nerves," I hear him tell his mother.

One evening, after a month passes, Tariq finds me by the telephone yet again. He strides toward me, picks up the phone and smashes the instrument against the corridor wall. Pieces of metal and wire emit trills as the instrument falls to the floor. "Enough!" he says, pushing his face close to mine. His voice is low, his breath hot on my cheeks. "People are inviting us out. Start acting the part."

I shrink back, terrified by his eyes, not understanding what caused him to change from a fatherly figure into a pacing tiger.

Seeing my fear, my husband's anger melts as quickly as it ignites. He holds my cheeks in his warm hands. "I'm sorry, my love. I didn't mean to frighten you. I want to see you happy. I'll buy you a new telephone, the best one in the market. You can go to 'Pindi tomorrow and visit your family. Don't be afraid."

After that explosion, I begin socializing with my husband beside me, reconciling myself to being the latest acquisition on his arm, wearing his rings and his surname. He likes to make late entrances at dinner parties with me dressed up, my throat bedecked with gold, rubies, and emerald pendants. After the twins are born, he thrives in the glow of having fathered two children, but he does not like to have my attention diverted. At his insistence, we continue going out at night, reveling in Karachi's party atmosphere under Ayub Khan, at a time when nightclubs and bars abound. The seventies have not started yet: the genocide in East Pakistan, the banning of alcohol, the closing of clubs, or the military coup and repression under General Zia's martial law.

Away from 'Pindi, I enjoy Karachi's cosmopolitan life. But my surface joy fades each time Tariq explodes. One time, he thrusts me to the bed, but I fall on the floor. Another time, I have bruises on my arm. Even his mother who lives upstairs notices my injuries and rallies to my side, cooking dishes for me, but she is too afraid to say anything to her eldest son. And I have no one, not even my sister, to talk to during that time.

Some days, I cannot drag myself out of bed, but other times, when Tariq's business is successful, he showers me with gifts and we invite friends to the house for parties, or we fly to London where he takes me shopping. During those times, he is the devoted husband, and my memory of his anger fades. Until the beast inside of him awakens. And then, I cannot remember the husband who massages my head, combs my hair, and covers my arms with kisses.

*   *   *

The room in which I stay is filled with Sameer's books, his video games, and his sneakers—a world distant from the one Yasmeen has left behind. Outside, the wind brushes against the oak, reminding me of Hawagali, a place where I found an escape from Tariq's swinging moods. I lived for the fresh air, rippling mountain streams, mist, and the daisies.

I dare not think of those Hawagali days. I have not returned to my family's mountain home since Yasir's death. Everything changed after that nightmarish night. Yasmeen is right. I left when a storm was brewing. But I had no idea that my son would step into the night to search for me.

*   *   *

In Hawagali, rain pours on my windscreen when I return home. The sky is dark, and my car's headlights shine on Tariq's car parked in our driveway. Heart racing, I turn off the car and step into the driveway, my kurta already drenched. My plait is undone and hair sticks to my forehead. I push open the front door and see Yasmeen in her nightgown, barefoot on the wooden stairs. Her forehead is burning hot.

"Why are you out of your bed?" I ask. I try to lead her to her bed, but she resists. "What's wrong?"

She shakes her head. "Yasir."

"Where is everyone?" I ask. "Where's Yasir? Abu? You need to get into bed. You'll catch pneumonia."

The front door flings open, blowing in mountain air, fresh after the thunderstorm. The cook, Saleem, stands in the doorway, holding a lantern, his shadow warped. Something is wrong, yet no one explains what has happened. In the distance, thunder crashes even though the rain has stopped.

My voice is high: "What's happening? Where is everybody?"

Saleem swings the lantern, distorting the shadows. "Yasir baba is gone."

I turn to Yasmeen. "What does he mean?"

Her toes curl on top of each other. "Abu's looking for Yasir." Her croaky voice reminds me of how sick she has been.

I take her hand. "You have to come to bed. I'll take care of everything."

I tuck her beneath her blanket and place a cold press upon her forehead. Her fever rages over 101 degrees, even though when I had left an hour ago, her temperature had dropped to normal. I'll have to call the doctor, I tell myself. My body is clammy. If I don't take care of myself, I, too, will be fever-ridden. I have to go downstairs and find out where my son is. "You lie down," I tell her. "I'll be back in a moment."

Downstairs, the house is deserted, but the wind swings the front door back and forth, its bumps corresponding with my heart. I step into the trickle of rain. In the distance I see lights moving like fireflies. The cars approach the house. Feeling like an Indian film actress in my wet clothes, I run outside. In the darkness, I discern Tariq's heavy voice. The taller figure is Saleem, and the bulky figure is the chowkidar, the night-watchman. Yasir is not in sight. I see another shadow and hear the words, "Doctorsahib" float in the air. The village doctor. I reach the men just as they step out of the cars. Tariq's hair is rumpled and his shalwar suit has mud-stains along his legs.

I laugh. "I'm glad you got the Doctorsahib. Yasmeen needs medicine to get strong."

Tariq doesn't return my laugh. He exchanges a glance with the doctor.

"Where is Yasir?"

No one answers. I hear the clip-clopping of a horse carriage behind them, its shape becoming visible through the fog. My heart leaps out of my body. "Where is my son?"

*   *   *

Shivering in Houston's damp air, I sit up, throw my shawl over my shoulders and grope my way down the staircase. I pour a glass of water and step outside for fresh air. A snail crawls by my feet and I watch it toil, keeling over beneath the weight of its shell, its tail leaving a silver thread in the moonlight.

On a similar night, a few months after the accident, I couldn't sleep. I woke up and wandered through our Karachi house. In the moonlight that filtered in from the drawing room's windows, I saw a sight that made me stop in my tracks: Yasmeen sat on the floor, her hands busy, shuffling and dealing out a pack of cards to an imaginary partner. Her open eyes were unseeing. I took her to a psychiatrist and he told me that Yasmeen had been sleepwalking since that July night.

Yasmeen stopped talking to us, and we accepted her grief. And when she got her college acceptances, we let her go.

She is right. There is more to tell, and I am ready to talk to her.

ten

YASMEEN

The doorbell rang and I scuttled downstairs, but Amman had opened the door to let Carlos in. Self-conscious under her scrutiny, I kissed Carlos' cheek and slipped into the kitchen to get drinks. Amman led him to the backyard where the children swam.

"Carlos! Swim with us!" Saira called from the pool.

"I'll wrestle you!" yelled Sam.

"Isn't it too cold to swim?" Amman asked.

"The pool's heated," Carlos reminded her.

Carlos knew. The heated pool was one of the luxuries that Jim had insisted on—much to my surprise—when we moved into the West University house. "Perfect for parties," he had said. Back then, Carlos had been a regular visitor to our year-round pool parties, and he and I had started our affair one evening much like this one, shortly after Carlos' break-up with his then-girlfriend. The parties stopped once Jim became the chair of his department, and our social life collapsed altogether.

Over splashes and squeals, I raised my voice to ask if I could help Amman make chicken tikkas, but she waved a prong in the air. "No, no—you relax. Today's my day for cooking. I hope this won't be too spicy for Carlos?"

She and I had not talked about my blowup a few nights ago, but under the warm sun and the sizzle of chicken, the tension between us had faded. That was the way of our family—no one ever resolved conflict.

Carlos sat at the edge, dangling his feet in the pool. Once he warmed up, he plunged in the water, with Sam slithering around him like an eel.

Saira's head popped out of the water. "Mom, you coming in?"

I dove in. The water stung my body, making me gasp and reemerge to slick wet hair off my forehead. In front of me paddled Carlos, his face alive with laughter. Tearing my eyes away, I pushed underwater and swam toward the penny at the bottom of the pool. Before I could grab it, another hand flicked the coin off the floor. Carlos. Underwater, relishing the feel of his arms, I wrestled him. Our faces heated, he and I broke the pool surface together with Amman and the kids watching us.

After dinner, we picked at the peach cobbler that Carlos had brought. He sat across from me, his rough-edged foot on mine as crickets chirped. Encouraged by food crumbs, a squirrel approached us. I placed my finger on my lips. Holding a breadcrumb, I dropped to the grass and slithered closer. The squirrel remained still as I approached, making guttural sounds. Once I dropped the bread on the ground, the squirrel snatched the crumb and clambered up a nearby tree, its tail flapping.

Saira clapped. "That was neat, Mom. How'd you make it stay so long?"

I shrugged. I had not tried my luck with an animal for some time.

Amman stacked the dishes. "Your mother's like that," she said.

"What do you mean?" Sam asked.

Amman waved her hand at me. "She's modest. She hasn't told you that she connects with animals? One time, we were at our vet's with our cat. A dog with rabies got loose. It was foaming at the mouth and no one knew what to do. Yasmeen went up to the animals one by one. She touched them and they fell quiet. She was able to calm the animals around us, so the vet and his assistants could capture the dog."

"Amman, you make me sound like a Doctor Doolittle or something!"

Amman's voice was proud. "The vet asked if she could be his assistant. But she was too young, of course. And remember the monkey story, Sir Bandir?"

"Monkey?" Both children sat up. "I want to know," they said in chorus.

A grin lurked on Carlos' lips.

Amman turned to Carlos. "That monkey story is one that is repeated in our family."

I didn't know whether to smile or to shout. I recognized the pattern: whenever she and Abu fought, they communicated through stories with Yasir and me.

Sam interrupted my thoughts. "Mom, you said you wanted to tell us more stories. But you never do!"

Saira scuffed the grass with her toes. "It's time for bed!" she mimicked my voice.

"Okay, okay." I melted as the sadness in Saira's voice reached me.

Carlos rubbed his hands together. "I want to hear this one, too..."

I didn't have to look at Amman to know that she, too, was waiting. Unable to resist the combined pressure that all four of them directed my way, I turned my chair to face the children, who lay sprawled on the grass. "All right! But you have to go to bed once I finish!"

* * *

One afternoon, when your Nani and my father were out of town, a young man named Hassan Khan stopped by our front gate to ask if we wanted to see a monkey show. His monkey, whose name was Sir Bandir, was dressed in the typical red waistcoat and tasseled hat that performance monkeys wore. My brother and I weren't allowed to let strangers into our house, but we had to bring Hassan into the driveway, especially after Sir Bandir jumped on my shoulder and began to whisper in my ear.

Hassan Khan's mouth opened and he said, "Sir Bandir has never done that with a stranger before!"

While I played with the monkey, Yasir, an expert at connecting with people, learned that Hassan Khan was from a village not far from Hawagali. He had found Sir Bandir injured from a car accident on his village street. Hassan Khan nursed the monkey back to health, and brought him to Karachi, where he heard there was a demand for monkey shows. "We have only been in Karachi two weeks. Business is more difficult than I thought." Hassan scratched his furrowed forehead.

Hearing Hassan's difficulties, Yasir ran upstairs and returned with five rupees, which he must have slipped out of our grandmother's purse.

The show began: Hassan narrated a story as Sir Bandir skipped up and down the driveway with his hands clasped behind his back as if he were strolling at the beach. The show ended with Sir Bandir writhing on the floor like a snake. His eyes closed and his body became still. Hassan peered into his pet's closed eyes for signs of life, but Sir Bandir did not move.

"Sir Bandir is dead," Hassan Khan announced, covering the monkey with a white cloth.

The moment Hassan lifted the cloth, Sir Bandir sprang to life, picking up his bowl into which I dropped money. Sir Bandir bowed and saluted and emptied the bowl in his master's lap.

Four days later, Hassan was at our door to report that since he had visited us, he had been hired by a rich man and would be doing shows for him on a regular basis. "It looks as if I may stay in Karachi after all," he said. "Performing for you brought me good fortune." He smiled and gave us a box of sweetmeats.

Hassan Khan and Sir Bandir became regular visitors, stopping by in the afternoons while grownups napped. One day, Hassan showed up without his usual whistle and smile. He had just received a telegram informing him that his father was sick.

"My family sent me money to catch the train to 'Pindi, but I can't take Sir Bandir with me," he said. "He gets sick on the ride."

Sir Bandir lay in the middle of our semi-circle, pretending to be dead. Only the gleam behind his half-open eyes and his undulating stomach revealed that he was awake and listening. Yasir and I exchanged glances, after which we both nodded. Yasir was on a mission to help those he could. A month earlier, he had given his allowance to our Bengali cook, so he could save towards visiting his family in the newly independent Bangladesh.

"Don't worry!" Yasir said. "We'll look after Sir Bandir. You know how good Yasmeen is with animals. You go home to see your father."

He pulled out rupees and coins from our piggy bank and stuffed the cash into Hassan Khan's pocket.

After Hassan left, Yasir and I retreated—with Sir Bandir clinging around my neck—to our hiding place beneath the banana tree grove where we made plans to keep Sir Bandir hidden in the servants' quarters that was not being used. We made a cot and fed Sir Bandir bananas that we sneaked out of the fruit bowl. Before leaving Sir Bandir, I talked to the monkey and explained that he had to be on his best behavior. Sir Bandir lay on his bedding and listened without chattering. I was certain that he understood me.

Over the next few days, Yasir and I perfected our schedule. Each day, after we returned from school and ate lunch, we made a show of consuming bananas and mangoes in front of our grandparents.

"You're getting so healthy," they marveled at our new healthy eating habits. They instructed our driver to buy more bananas, mangoes, and grapes for us, which we packed and carried to Sir Bandir.

As the days wore on, Yasir and I adjusted to our routine of feeding Sir Bandir in the mornings before school and in the afternoons once we returned. After lunch, while grownups slept, we slipped to the servants' room where we hid Sir Bandir. Wrapping the monkey in cloth, we placed him in a straw basket and carried him to the banana grove. There, we let him hop around. Sir Bandir seemed to understand the need for secrecy; he kept his chatter to a whisper and remained close to us. Our plan seemed foolproof, and we were sure that Sir Bandir would remain undetected as long as we needed.

Ten days after Sir Bandir moved into our home, a strike near our school delayed our return from school. We reached home two hours later than our usual time. As soon as the driver turned off the car engine, we heaved our satchels over our shoulders and leapt out of the car. I told Yasir to greet our grandparents while I checked on Sir Bandir. But when I entered the dark room, I was greeted by silence. My eyes fell on a hole in the window netting—one that hadn't been there before. I hurried outside to peer at the trees above.

"Sir Bandir," I hissed. "I know you're there. Come to me!" But the only response I got was from a crow in the neem tree.

By the time Yasir appeared on the upstairs balcony to call me for lunch, he knew what had happened. I hurried up the stairs, knowing that we would have to figure out a way to find Sir Bandir after we finished our lunch. The moment our plates were cleared, we kissed our grandmother's papery cheek, and raced downstairs to circle the grounds again.

Dishes rattled in the upstairs kitchen and distant shouts emanated from boys playing cricket on the street. As we looked around, we heard another sound: a squeak from the next door mosque, signaling that the loudspeaker and microphone had been turned on. The mullah cleared his throat and started his prayer.

On cue, our grandmother, Dadi, emerged from her room to walk along the upper balcony to the tap where she performed ablutions five times a day. She dropped out of our view as she deposited herself on her wooden stool, but we could picture her. We had seen her ritual many times.

Yasir tugged at my sleeve and pointed to the almond tree branches that shaded Dadi's balcony. Sir Bandir sat on a branch observing Dadi. I ran beneath the tree trunk, holding out a banana as bait. As we watched, Sir Bandir extended one hairy arm away from his body, rubbing the fingers from his other hand. He did the same with his left hand. I knew he was imitating Dadi's prayer preparation.

"Sir Bandir," I whispered.

Sir Bandir bent his head toward us. He hopped off a low-hanging branch onto the balcony wall to tower over Dadi's head.

"Oh, no," Yasir and I breathed. We could barely see the top of Dadi's head, but from the way Sir Bandir held his long-toed foot in the air, we guessed that Dadi was washing her feet. I held my breath and closed my eyes. I didn't want to see what would happen next.

"AAaaaieeeeee!" Dadi's voice ricocheted through the air.

I opened my eyes. Dadi stood on her wooden stool with her arms in the air as if she were in a bank holdup. Sir Bandir, on the balcony wall in front of Dadi, raised his hands too. We heard a clatter from the kitchen. The cook Masi had dropped the pot she was washing. She entered the balcony and expelled a shriek when she saw Sir Bandir. Picking up a jharroo—a twig broom—she charged toward Sir Bandir, who leapt off the balcony wall back onto the tree branch. Watched by Sir Bandir, Masi helped Dadi off her stool.

With Dadi away from the wall, Masi flapped the jharroo at Sir Bandir. He copied her action without a broom in his hand. Scratching his chest, he opened his jaw and let out a screech. Masi dropped her broom and clamped her hands on her ears. Sir Bandir copied her. He grinned and held out his hand in Dadi's direction, but Dadi's gray eyebrows were furrowed. Sir Bandir reclaimed his hand and scratched his chin.

Dadi strode up to Sir Bandir and stopped in front of him so that the eighteen-inch monkey on the balcony and her four feet ten-inch frame were face to face. Opening her mouth, she belted out a stream of Urdu curse words: "Kutta, kamina, ganda, ghaliz, haramjada!" When finished, she turned on her heel and strode to her bedroom that adjoined the balcony.

This time, Sir Bandir didn't copy her actions. Instead, he hid his head under his elbow. Dadi had won the round.

* * *

I stretched my arms and observed the children's smiles.

"Whoo! Whoo! I'm a monkey!" exclaimed Sam. He hopped on the grass, his elbows pushed out, fists tucked under his arms, and lips extended in a pout.

Behind me, Amman broke into a laugh. "Baita, this story's been told to me many times—by many different people. But I've never heard it told so well."

Saira spoke up. "But what happened to the monkey? You forgot that part."

I stood up and took her hand. "Time for bed. I'll answer your question once I tuck you in."

As soon as she lay down, Saira asked, "So? What happened?"

"Dadi told the driver to take Sir Bandir to the zoo. But the driver liked the monkey so much that he persuaded one of his relatives to look after Sir Bandir until Hassan returned to Karachi. So everything worked out."

"And did you get in trouble?"

"Yasir and I weren't allowed to spend time together for three days—but that didn't matter too much because we could communicate with each other without talking."

"How come we never have cool pets?" Sam asked. "I want monkeys!"

"We'll go to Karachi—I promise you can see all the monkey and cobra snake shows that you want."

"When can we go?" Sam demanded.

"Soon." I kissed them and walked to the door.

"Mom—wait!" Saira called.

"Yes?" My mind had drifted to Carlos and Amman outside. I wondered what they were talking about.

"Did your brother talk to animals? You know, like you did?"

I held on to the doorpost. "Not really…"

"How come?"

"He liked animals, but they weren't drawn to him the way animals came to me. He didn't mind. He knew that was my gift. He was better with people."

"Mom," Saira's voice was a whisper and I could hear her tiredness. "One more thing?"

I sat down next to her and caressed her hair. "Yes?"

"Is Carlos your boyfriend?"

I was glad the room was dark. "Would you like that?"

"Yeah," called Sam from his bed. "He's cool. Dad has a girlfriend, so you should have a boyfriend."

I smiled, wishing I could approach life with a child's logic. "Good night, little ones."

Without pushing for response, the children allowed me to leave the room.

* * *

I walked Carlos to his car, my hand brushing against his. "So—what stories did Amman tell you?"

"She wasn't sharing any secrets. Just political stuff. She's well-informed. I didn't know that the US government had such deep ties to your dead dictator, Zia. She was talking about how Reagan groomed the Taliban."

I nodded. "The Afghan militants were called Mujahideen at that time. Those were tough times in our history, and the Reagan government supported Pakistan's worst dictator. No one ever cared to know much about Pakistan. Until now."

"I'm always interested."

I slipped into his arms. "This evening I've been thinking about your lips more than about politics." I snaked my tongue inside his mouth and he responded with the same. "I want to go to your house—with you."

Carlos laughed. "You sure? I don't want you disappearing tomorrow."

I answered his question by wrapping my arms around him.

At his house, Carlos and I kissed each other, feeling no urgency to throw ourselves on the bed. We fell asleep with our legs tangled together, but I awoke at two in the morning and nudged Carlos. "I have to get home..."

He rolled over, squashing me with his weight. "Just stay. I'll drive you back next year. Or maybe the one after." His voice was thick with sleep.

I sat up. "I didn't tell anyone I was here. They'll worry."

In the car, I told Carlos about my conversation with Henrietta.

"She wants me to attend a San Francisco conference. How am I going to juggle the kids and the conference? Jim's out of town, and so are the Millers. And Amman leaves next week."

He looked at me. "San Francisco? That should be fun!"

My face heated up. "I suppose I could ask Amman to stay longer."

Carlos pulled the car to a stop in the driveway and turned off the headlights. "Why not? Your kids love to spend time with her, right?"

"I hate going to new places alone..."

Carlos scratched his chin. "Funny you should say that. I'm done planning my spring classes and was thinking of visiting my aunt in the Bay Area. If you invite me..."

"What the hell!" I nodded. "Sure. I'd love it."

"We could dine in my old hangouts. I'll go see my friends. Wait for you in bed. I promise I won't distract you. Not too much."

My belly curled at the thought of him waiting for me.

"Think about it. Don't say yes under the full moon and regret it later. Because you'll have to talk to me after we return to Houston."

eleven

YASMEEN

After dinner in San Francisco's Mission District, Carlos and I took a stroll to work off our burritos meal. I drew out my cigarette case and lit one, but the nicotine tasted rancid. I handed the pack to a panhandler.

As we passed a hotel, Carlos laughed. "When we were kids, we used to sneak into that building and pull the fire alarms. Sometimes, doormen caught us and chased us around the building. I was a street kid." His tone changed as he took my hand to lead me to a bakery at a street corner, its racks filled with layered cakes.

"Our family had to sell the bakery when my parents died. I don't want to know who owns it now." The bakery's name had changed from Rios Bakers to Cakes Galore.

In the afternoon, Carlos drove towards his aunt's house. With our windows rolled down, I opened my mouth, swallowing air, unsure of the visit that lay ahead. Two weeks ago, if someone had told me that I would spend a weekend with Carlos in his home city while Amman cared for the children in Houston, I would have laughed. But reality could not be disputed. Carlos was showing me his childhood haunts and introducing me to his family, while I trusted my mother with grandchildren whom she had met less than a month ago.

Carlos' voice cut through my thoughts. "My aunt's a traveler. She wants to hear about Pakistan. Call her María. Like I do." He parked the rented car on a shaded street and entered a three-story building.

Before we could reach the top to ring the bell, the door flung open and a round-faced woman with jet-black hair held out her arms. She ruffled Carlos' hair and held him for a few moments. Turning to me, María said, "Welcome! Welcome! I've heard a lot about you. Muy bonita!" she added, turning to Carlos. "Just like you said."

We stepped into the apartment's open room lit by bay windows that were flung open. One wall was decorated with Mexican tapestries. In a corner, inside a hanging cage, sat a red and green parrot who was introduced to me as Lobo. Dinner consisted of corn tortillas and chicken in home made mole sauce, a family recipe, which I devoured, comfortable with María who switched between Spanish and English, telling us about the students at the school where she taught.

"I wish they could meet you. I tell them grades don't matter. They have to have the desire to do well. You weren't the best student, but look at you now, professor!"

A bookshelf showcased black and white family photographs, including one of a short woman in a flowing dress with her arm hooked to that of a mustached man in a suit. Carlos picked up the image, dusted it, and set it back down. "My parents." He chose another photograph, one with a boy holding a football larger than his face.

"My dad loved to coach me."

He cut a slice of homemade cake and winked at María. "My dad knew everything. He taught María how to bake killer cakes."

María threw her head back and laughed. "Your dad learned from me. When we were little, he and I played in our mom's kitchen. That's how we learned. But I showed him how to improve." María nodded towards me. "Carlos was a pain when I was younger. He chased away all my dates. Only after Carlos left for college did my first husband find the courage to propose to me."

Carlos grinned. "Someone had to look out for you. Those hombres were no good. One time, our family organized a picnic at Muir Woods. María brought a boyfriend along. For some reason, the man wore a blazer—I don't know where he thought we were going. He sweated the whole afternoon. After our meal, he invited María to join him for a walk in the forest. I found them just when he had dropped on his knees to propose to her. I picked up a stone and threatened to split his forehead open if he didn't let her go. He started to hiccup and wasn't able to stop until we reached San Francisco."

I laughed. Jim's family had never been so relaxed.

"So, you go back to your country often?" María asked, pouring more tea.

I fed the parrot a sprig of celery. "Not that much."

"She hasn't been in eighteen years," Carlos interjected. "Not since she flew to the US to attend college."

I glanced out of the window, hoping he would drop the subject.

María's eyes moved between my face and Carlos'. "I wanted to learn more about your culture. I teach middle school, and my students are from around the globe, including Afghanistan and Pakistan. One Afghan boy was beaten up. They tell me their dads are getting laid off. Is that happening in Houston also?"

"Some. My mother's visiting and she's talked to her—our—relatives around the US. They share stories about arrests, deportations, and layoffs. Many are returning to Pakistan, or migrating to Canada or another country that will take them."

"If I saw you on the street, I wouldn't know where you were from," María said. "You could be Mexican, South American, Greek..."

María's observations were familiar. My ability to blend was a gift that I relished as strangers tried to identify my origins. Urdu was the first language I spoke, but I didn't articulate the words often, not even with Amman, especially since my formal education had been in English. When we married, Jim said that he used to hear me mumble words in my sleep that he didn't recognize, but I never knew whether I was talking in Urdu or if I had invented my own language.

"What do you say when people ask you where you're from?" María asked. "Do you tell them you're Pakistani or do you say you're American?"

I walked over to the parrot and stroked its beak. "I'm not really American." My tone made her stop asking me any more questions.

*   *   *

Carlos' breath fluttered the sheet against my neck. I rolled away feeling sweaty, but when I tossed the covers off, goose-bumps rose up along my arms. I got out of bed to brush my teeth a second time, an action that fooled my body to slip into sleep mode. Shuffling back to the bed, I sat on the edge and watched Carlos' back undulate.

Moonlight slipped in through open curtains. I picked up my robe, smooth against my body, and padded toward the French doors. The wind on the balcony cooled my cheeks. Mist clung to my face and hands. My heart beat fast. Something was going to happen.

Clouds wrapped around me, making it difficult for me to see beyond my outstretched hand. Drizzle began to splatter on the balcony floor and the iron rail. I patted my bare feet on the wet floor as my mother used to do, the water and mist making me feel as if I were in Hawagali on the night Yasir left us. I shivered, remembering my fever, the temperature making me more mercurial, porous. That night I felt as if I could slither into Amman's mind, read her thoughts. She was troubled—troubled about more than my sickness.

My elbows dug into my ribs and my wet robe that clung to my body. Mist swirled around me just as Yasir had experienced on the night of his accident, a few months after we turned seventeen, smothering him forever. Where had Amman gone that night, and why did she say goodbye to me? I paced the balcony floor. The mist cocooned me like a blanket, carrying me to the night that still made no sense.

*   *   *

Thunder crashes, making me shiver in my Hawagali bed. My feverish mind travels through walls and closed doors, soaking in Abu's voice. I hear him throw an object. Closing my eyes, I picture my parents' room where Amman cowers by the dressing table.

I lose focus and drift out of the room. Their voices slip away from my consciousness. In my bed, I close my eyes. I know Abu will hurt Amman. I try to slide off the bed, but I am paralyzed. More voices: Amman's soft like a river; his, harsh like hailstorm rattle. I fade into sleep once they fall silent. When their door opens, I smell her jasmine perfume. She enters my room, and I welcome her with a cracked smile.

Placing her palm on my forehead, Amman says: "I'm going to bring you an ice-pack. Your fever is still high."

In the kitchen, she rattles pots and dishes. The cook must have stepped away for a tea with the night-watchman, the chowkidar. Through my delirium, I visualize Abu sleeping in his bedroom, Amman working in the kitchen, and Yasir napping in the attic. He likes to be in bed during rainstorms. The lamps around the house are lit even though a few hours remain before nightfall.

Amman reenters my room with a bowl of ice and towelettes.

"Is everything okay?" I ask.

"Of course!" she says. "And why shouldn't it be?" Sitting beside me, Amman places cool towels on my forehead and my eyes. I lie with my chest rising and falling. Amman places her face on my stomach, barely touching me. She brushes off her tears and picks up a towel from my forehead, replacing it with another fresh one.

"My little one," she whispers. She paces the room, whispering words that I can't decipher. At my desk, she tears paper from my sketch-pad. I open my eyes to see her scribbling. She is writing—not drawing. Amman doesn't often write, preferring to express herself through song or drawings. When she turns around and sees my eyes pinned on her, she crumples the paper and throws it in the corner of the room.

Returning to my side, she lifts the towel from my forehead and inserts a thermometer in my mouth, tracking time with her watch. Ripples of sweat roll down my forehead and soak the sheets. My fever has broken.

Amman helps me walk to a chair and strips the bed sheets. She changes my pillow cases and tucks in fresh sheets. Once finished with the bed, she helps me out of my pajamas and dresses me in a fresh pair, the cotton cool against my skin. We don't exchange words, but I am aware of Amman's tears behind her eyes.

She walks me into bed. "You're better now," she whispers from the doorway. "I'm going to check on your father."

When she returns, her jasmine perfume is heavier. I awaken as her lips rest on my forehead. Amman's hair is pulled back and she wears a maroon kurta with a blue border, one that I love. But I don't understand why she is dressed up.

"I'm going out for a little while, Baita," she says. "I'll be with Heera. I promised that I would visit her. You need to rest. I'll be back very soon."

A roll of thunder jerks my eyes open. Amman is in the doorway, surveying me. Her eyes are dark as if her pupils are filled with black ink. She approaches me and kisses me again. "Sleep. I'll be home soon. This time I will come home."

Only after I hear the car drive away do I wonder why she says, "This time..."

My bare feet were numb on the stone balcony and my teeth chattered, making my chin feel as if it were going to fall off. I pulled open the French door and reentered the hotel room. The armchair was closer than the bed, and I dropped on the seat. Carlos was asleep, curled up on his side like a boy.

The note that Amman crumpled in my room. Who was she writing to? Why weren't servants around? I shivered and pulled my nightgown around me, the wet silk cold against my skin. A few feet away, Carlos' body and the comforter beckoned me, but I could not heave myself off the chair.

I sleep more. Yasir enters my room. The sun has set, and rain pelts against the roof. The smell of wet earth rises from the ground to saturate my nostrils.

"Feeling better?" Yasir asks. "Abu says I should give you some soup."

"Where's Amman?"

He shrugs. "She took the car. Should be back soon—it's almost seven."

"She's driving?" I'm wide-awake. My fever has gone, but I'm exhausted.

"She went to see Heera in the village. Maybe I'll walk there to see if she wants me to drive back. You know how she can't see at night. She always forgets her glasses."

His laughter is hearty as if he is at a party, while mine is crackly as if a twig is caught in my throat. The kerosene lamp that Yasir lights illuminates his flushed cheeks. Tufts of his curly hair are alive in the humidity, making him look taller in the shadowy light.

I duck under the sheets when a strip of lighting crackles and lights the room. Normally I love thunderstorms, but this one frightens me. If lightning strikes close, the house will ignite, spreading fire into the surrounding forest.

Yasir disappears into the attic. For a moment, I wonder why he went upstairs if he plans to go out. Unlike me, Yasir is afraid of thunderstorms, and he usually recedes into his bed when he hears thunder.

Footsteps resound in the hall, distracting me from my thoughts. Abu's figure, shorter than Yasir's, fills the doorway. "Is your mother back?" he asks.

I shrink under my cover. From the corner of my eye, I notice a crumpled ball of paper that Amman tossed to the side. I tell myself not to draw attention to it.

*   *   *

"Yasmeen?" Across the room, Carlos patted the empty side of the bed. He sat up and looked around the room, and leapt up to hold me in his arms. "You cried out. What's going on?"

I shook my head against his chest.

He placed his hand on my forehead. "You're sick—your body feels hot."

"I'm fine," I whispered. Yasir raced into the rain to find Amman. He returned, his body flat in a horse carriage.

"I'm going to the lobby to get something for your fever."

I shake my head. My teeth would not stop chattering. He would not return. Carlos would get lost in the fog like Yasir did.

Carlos wrapped a blanket around me. "Sshh... You'll be fine." He led me to the bed and changed me out of my wet clothes.

I fell asleep before he could even tuck blankets around me.

twelve

LAILA

The doorbell chimes. I set the newspaper down and peer out of the window. Janet's car is parked in the driveway. She has been dropping by during the evenings to make sure I don't need anything. On several occasions, she drove me to the grocery store. I check my wristwatch and note that Janet has stopped by in the middle of the day. I wonder why she's not at her office. When I open the door, I notice that her forehead is furrowed.

In the kitchen, I place a kettle on the stove to prepare tea.

Janet paces the room, holding a scrap of paper between her fingers.

"Is everything all right?" I ask.

She thrusts the paper toward me. "This is the number where Yasmeen can be reached. Carlos called. He is in San Francisco with her. He said she's contracted double pneumonia. She's in a hospital."

My hand remains on my chest.

Janet presses my shoulder. "She's been on IV since early morning. I wanted to tell you in person."

"IV?"

"Drips, as you say."

I straighten my kurta and stand up. My daughter is sick and I am far from her. I picture Yasmeen's face, eyes shut, her breath slipping away. I grab my purse and stride toward the door.

Janet follows. "Where are you going?"

"Please drive me to the airport," I whisper. I have to be with her." My only child. Yasir's crumpled body lies behind me, his life thrown away. And now Yasmeen...

Janet's fingers are on my elbow. "Mrs. Akeel—Laila—the doctors have said that she'll be okay."

"You're a mother. You understand." Each syllable I utter is a rock that I have to force out of my throat. "I have to be with her." Yasmeen, her arms pierced with needles pumping vitamins into her failing system. Yasmeen, alone, far away from our home.

"Carlos will fly back with her—in a few days. As soon as the doctors release her." Her eyes meet mine. "She will be fine."

"I have to be with her."

Janet draws me into the kitchen. "Let's call first."

"My son had pneumonia." He died. But I cannot utter those words. Not out loud, not again.

"This is different. If they say that her condition is serious, I'll take you to the airport, and I'll look after the children." Janet picks up the house telephone and dials a number.

Carlos' voice is on the other end. "Mrs. Akeel—Laila—don't worry. She'll be fine. Your daughter's a fighter."

"I want to be with her." Yasmeen is my only child and no one can understand. Much as Yasmeen's friends love her, they cannot understand our ways. We do not leave the care of our loved ones to doctors and nurses, not unless we're prepared to lose them. I picture Jinnah hospital's private rooms where family members take turns to be with loved ones. The general wards are crowded. Men and women eat and sleep for days on the floors beside the beds of their family members. I remember when Kaneez Bua was sick. We admitted her into Civil Hospital—no one put servants into the fancy hospitals—and I went into the general wards to visit her. Both her daughters sat on the floor beside the bed, waiting for the doctor.

Carlos' voice is louder. "She's fine, Mrs. Akeel. She's smiling in her sleep. She knows I'm talking to you."

Sweat from my palm mingles with tears. I feel as if the Arabian Sea has moved in between my ears. "I have to go." My voice is a whisper.

Janet leads me to a chair and prepares tea for me. "We'll call the airlines. I'll take the children to my house."

The children. They will return from school in a few hours. I have to prepare their snack and walk to the end of the street to meet them.

Janet places her hand on my arm. "If you want to be with Yasmeen, the children can stay with me. They have before. I'll pick them up from school and take them to my house. They'll be fine."

I lift my dupatta toward my eyes as if the fabric were a sieve for my tears.

*　　*　　*

In San Francisco's maze-like Pacific Medical Center, a white-coated nurse guides me down a corridor. My teeth chatter, and I pull my coat closer to my body wondering why air-conditioning is on during wintertime. Once at Yasmeen's door, I enter the room. On the far side, by the window on a second bed, lies Yasmeen, her chest undulating. I walk toward her to drop a kiss on her cheek.

Her eyelashes flutter open. "Amman," she says. Her voice is a croak. Holding her free hand, I place her palm on my cheek, but she has dropped back to sleep.

Carlos is curled up on the sofa beside the bed. He sits up to wipe the side of his mouth when he hears me. "Glad you could be here. She's on sedatives so she can rest after being awake all night. Her chest hurt, and she coughed mucous and blood. But the doctors do say she will be fine."

I set my overnight bag next to the bed, deposit myself on a chair, and draw out my knitting needles. Yasmeen will have another sweater by the time she wakes up. Carlos' eyes are red, his body crumpled. He leaves for his hotel to get some rest once I'm settled in the room.

In a room that smells of antiseptic cleaners, I focus on counting stitches, trying to push away alternating pictures of Yasir and Yasmeen—both lying in bed, faces pale, eyes refusing to open. I remember how I squeezed Yasir's hand, breathed into his face, hoping that I could bring life back into his body.

*　　*　　*

Long after the thunderstorm ends, after Tariq and the doctor bring Yasir to the house, I sit beside him. Hidden beneath a blanket, Yasir's body barely fits on the bed, his feet extending over the edge. Pressing his hand to my cheek, I mumble prayers I have not uttered in a long time, breathing heat into his palm, urging his sickness to leave his chest, his heart. In the room next door, Yasmeen rests, her fever gone.

Doctor-sahib places his stethoscope on Yasir's chest, his forehead furrowed as he strains to listen to Yasir's heart. "Keep him warm," he says. "Hot water bottles, tea. Anything to increase his heartbeat."

Tariq stands beside me, alcohol and anger melted from his system. He combs my hair with his fingers and kisses the crown of my head. "Sorry," he mumbles. "I swear I'll never treat you like that again."

I remain silent.

"I promise. I'll never hurt any of you again." Tariq's voice is a whisper. His face is unshaven and his eyes red. Even his mustache droops. He wanders to the kitchen, returning with three hot water bottles. Together we lift up Yasir's body to slide the bottles beneath his back, neck, and on his heart. Yasir's eyes remain closed.

Wearing her flannel nightgown, Yasmeen enters the room to push past us. She throws herself on her twin. Holding his hands between hers to warm them, she cries, "Wake up, Yasir!"

Her tears spill on his heart, the golden heart that we forget when he disappears for hours in the attic. She breathes into her brother's chest, but Yasir remains still, his face pale like the one belonging to the fairy tale prince who freezes. Unlike characters in the stories that he and his twin read, Yasir does not awaken.

At dawn, Doctorsahib covers Yasir's face with a white sheet. Yasmeen drops on the floor beside Yasir's bed. Afraid that she might harm herself, the doctor sedates her and then me.

*   *   *

The only light in the room is a white sliver that slides in beneath the door. Yasmeen moans in her sleep. I stroke her back, trying to calm her breath. Finally, tired of staring into the darkness, not being able to stare past Yasir's dead eyes to find Yasmeen's living ones, I walk in circles around the room, knitting in the dark. The clicking of my needles is the beat of a train transporting my fear to saner thoughts.

Having had the night to process my thoughts, I wonder how Carlos is with Yasmeen on her business trip. Perhaps her relationship with Carlos is related to her divorce. Flinching in the dark, I drop a stitch. Is it a family curse: Women marrying men they don't love while maintaining relationships with men they love but do not marry?

Hawagali's purple heather fields beneath fast-moving clouds flood my memories as I remember the summer when Yasir left us.

*　　*　　*

I lean against the oak tree, surrounded by marigolds, daisies, and chrysanthemums. The air is heavy with the drone of bees. Yasir lies on his back staring at clouds, a blade of grass in his mouth. Yasmeen sits across from him, her fingers flying as she fills her page with a sketch of her twin. Their father has decided to stay in Karachi. "Too much work," he says. We shrug off his apology but no one is too upset. Life is calmer without his temper and bootlegged whiskey.

"Why can't you leave him?" Yasir asks. His voice is usually low-pitched, but these days, he sounds cranky because his father has been trying to force our son to study business so Yasir can take over family cotton and sugar factories. When in Karachi, Yasir and Tariq have heated exchanges a few times a week. Tariq shoves Yasir, sometimes striking his chest, or sometimes tapping Yasir's shoulder. Each time, Yasir's eyes narrow. One day, Yasir will strike his father back. Until then, Yasir's anger recedes behind his eyes where nothing—except Yasmeen, his writing, and his smoking—can reach him.

I fix my eyes on my teacup.

"You could follow your heart?" His voice is insistent.

"My heart. What do you know about my heart?" I feel as if a stone rests upon my chest.

Yasir props himself up. I hear paper crackle. The smell of cigarettes or perhaps something stronger seeps out from his pants' pocket. I look away from his deep gaze. "Go with your heart, Amman. Leave Abu. Follow your heart."

I set my teacup down with a clink.

His eyebrows are joined. "You've already left him…"

Goosebumps race along my arms. I stand up. "I must check up on our dinner."

Yasir hurls his body onto the grass. Slipping a fresh blade of grass between his lips, he hums a tune that I cannot recognize. And a month later, one of us does depart in a manner no one could have predicted.

* * *

I turn around. Yasmeen has regained consciousness. Her eyes meet mine.

"Amman," she says, opening her arms, inviting me to hold her.

thirteen

YASMEEN

I soar over verdant Hawagali mountains. High above, monkeys screech my name. Yasir pushes through mist that clings to the fuzz above his lip as he returns from Heera's house without Amman. When rain descends, he uses his umbrella's prong to guide him forward on the path he knows well. Struggling up the mountain road, he avoids the tumbling branches and rocks that are pushed by the rain.

Yasir's foot lands on a rock that sends pain up his left ankle. His umbrella slips out of his grip, and he falls on the slick paved road. Forcing himself up, he massages his ankle, grabs his umbrella, and hurtles forward, determined to fight the rain. Thunder rumbles. God moving his furniture, we used to say. On this mountain slope in Hawagali, Yasir never doubts that there are gods and goddesses watching him, protecting him, leading him home.

Rain lashes against his cheeks, but Yasir moves forward, not realizing how close he is to the edge of the road. Out of breath, he leans against a fir tree trunk and digs his umbrella point into the ground. Water streams down his nose into his shirt collar, soaking his vest. The curving path home—which he knows like the arch of his nose—will lead to our house.

"Ten minutes away," Yasir breathes. His twisted ankle will slow his pace. In the darkness, he trips on an oak tree root and falls. This time, the umbrella-walking stick cascades down the slope. He forces himself to rise, pushing from tree to tree against the horizontal rain, doubling his body to maintain balance on one leg. After he passes the sculptor's cottage to his left, he knows he'll reach the forked road from where our house is a few hundred yards away.

From my bed, half a mile away, I whisper, "Yasir, just come home. Don't lose hope." I want him to hear me, but my spirit is weak. I float above, watching him battle the rain. He limps. One two, one two forward.

His foot, the one with the damaged ankle, slips on a patch of pine needles. He falls. This time, he cannot stand up. Cobra plants twine around his legs and pin him down while kaneezes swoop over his face, their irises gleaming in the rain. Yasir rolls three feet down the hillside. He grabs a tree trunk.

"Hold on," I breathe. "Wait till the rain halts." But cobra plants wind around his arms, legs, and torso, refusing to release him. Yasir loses his balance on the incline and rolls with rainwater down the hillside, gathering momentum. His ribs snap, and his legs crack as his body twists in the river of rain.

"Hold on, Yasir, don't give up."

A pine tree arrests his fall. He lies on the slope, limp and silent.

*   *   *

I struggled to sit up, but was held back by tubes and straps on my chest. Needles attached to my wrist prevented me from moving my arm.

"You're okay." Amman sat beside to me, holding my hand.

Shaking my head, I tried to remember. Maybe Yasir's accident was a nightmare, and the years in between were part of a dream. I registered the hospital room that smelled of antiseptics. A man hovered by my bed. Carlos. My time felt like jumbled yarn: Hawagali, Carlos, the hotel balcony, mist, and rain.

Carlos moved closer.

Amman said, "Do you remember anything? Let me bring you some soup. And once the hospital releases you, I can cook my special recipe in Houston. We need to get you back to your normal self. Skin and bones." She exited the room, shaking her head.

Carlos rolled up the bed ramp, so I could sit up.

"The children?" I asked.

"With Janet. They're fine."

My arms had blue veins sticking out. "I don't understand what happened."

"You'll remember soon enough. You're on a lot of meds right now."

My chest hurt, and my shoulder blades felt as if pine needles were poking into my back. "Was I sleepwalking?" The last image I remembered was Yasir in the rain. Something else sat in the crevice of my memory but I couldn't retrieve the thought.

Carlos squeezed my hand. "Don't worry chiquita. You'll remember soon enough."

Amman bustled in with a tray, and Carlos returned my hand. I forced myself to swallow one spoonful of soup at a time, conscious of my dead taste buds. Finally, unable to eat more, I pushed the bowl away.

After Amman left the room to put away the tray, Carlos leaned forward to kiss my shoulder. "We were worried. You were almost frozen when I woke up."

A thought struck me. "Carlos—what did you tell Amman?"

He raised his eyebrows.

"About you? Being here with me? In San Francisco."

"I didn't know I needed to say anything."

I raised my eyebrows.

"I called Janet—she told your mom." Carlos laughed. "No one cares that we were together! We're just relieved that you're okay."

* * *

Janet pulled up in the driveway, and Carlos helped me out of the car. Saira's face was streaked with tears. She gripped the rose stems that she had brought to the airport. Hovering close to me, she helped me walk inside, while Sam picked up my hand luggage. In the sunlight, the street looked the same: green and shaded. No neighbors were in sight. From a distance floated the tune of the ice-cream cart, drowning the roar of a lawn mower. Newspapers wrapped in plastic were piled on one of our neighbor's driveways. They, too, must have been away. Sights and sounds were familiar, yet I felt as if I had changed.

Once I was tucked in bed, my tears flowed unchecked; the children were unpacking their belongings in their room.

"I feel so weak," I whispered. Carlos held me close.

"I don't want the children to see me like this." Mucous streamed down my nose, and I mopped it up against my sleeve. "I don't even sound like myself."

When I awakened, Carlos was gone, and Amman sat on the chair knitting. She leapt up when I opened my eyes. "I'm going to heat up more soup!"

*　*　*

She presses towels on my forehead and leans over to kiss my cheeks. "You must get better," she whispers.

My head lolls on my pillow. Yasir is upstairs in the Hawagali attic, where Amman and Shireen Khala once played hide-and-seek with Babur. Through closed eyes, I see Yasir pacing the ground, tired of the rain. He wants to be outside riding on a horse, chasing the wind.

Leaping down the stairs, he appears by my door. "What're we doing for dinner?" he asks.

"We'll eat in a little while." Amman leaves for her room. With my eyes closed, I can see her in front of her mirror, combing her hair. Yasir picks up my arm and moves his fingers as if he were playing the guitar that he yearns to own. A car roars up the driveway. We hear a door slam. Abu's voice rumbles through the house.

Yasir stiffens. "What's *he* doing here? He wasn't supposed to be in Hawagali." He pushes past my bed. "I don't want to see him. I'm going up."

Through my fever, I see Amman's hand frozen on her comb, locked in her tangled hair.

*　*　*

Saira peered around the door, followed by Sam. I stretched my arms, and they flung themselves on the bed. With hands too weak to lift even a coffee cup, I caressed and kissed their foreheads.

"I'm okay," I murmured.

Saira's sobs grew louder. Janet had told me how, after hearing about my hospitalization, Saira hadn't stopped crying and that she had talked in her sleep, calling out to me.

Remembering the doctor's comment on how I would not have survived my bout of pneumonia had Carlos not rushed me to the emergency room, I could not stop thinking about Yasir, and about how no one had been able to do the same for him.

The children came into my room and sat on the carpet drawing with Amman. In a corner armchair, Carlos read a magazine. As bedtime approached, the children got up to brush their teeth, and returned to kiss me goodnight.

Sitting by my feet, Saira said, "I have to tell you a story. I'll tell Sam another one when we're in bed. Nani said that was okay. Can you listen to my story today?"

I smiled. "I'd love to hear your story, little one."

She cleared her throat. "Well, this is a story that Nani told us when you were away. The story is different from the ones that I read—it's set in the mountains of Pakistan.

"One day, Nani was playing in her mountain house. It was cold and windy, and her doll started talking to her, telling her that Nani had to help the gatekeeper's daughter, Heera. So Nani tried to find a magic flower, but she didn't have any luck. She asked her mother, instead, to get help for Heera so Heera could walk again. You see, Heera had been struck with an illness called polio. Nani's mother helped. She put Heera in a hospital, and when Heera returned to Hawagali, she could walk again, but she had a limp.

"The next day, the mountain house was bathed in mist and fog, Nani and her friend Heera found a magic mountain and they climbed to the top together. Nani was happy because she was able to help Heera walk again, and both girls were happy because they became best friends. The end."

"That's a lovely story." I kissed my daughter and caught Amman's smile.

Saira snuggled closer.

Once Amman took the kids to bed, Carlos stood up and stretched. "You don't mind the stories anymore."

I nodded. "Actually, I want Amman to tell me a few stories. She needs to answer some questions." I closed my eyes. I could wait.

*   *   *

I was alone in my room when my telephone rang.

"Just calling to see how you are," Jim's voice greeted me. Since our custody battle, Jim and I had limited our telephone and in-person conversations, preferring to communicate via email or handwritten notes passed to each other through the children. "Molly sends her regards."

"Say hello to her," I responded, trying to maintain a level tone.

"So what happened? I'm concerned that you left my children without proper care."

"They were with my mother and then with Janet," I ignored his referral to the children as being his. "They've stayed with Janet before—while we were together. Remember?" I couldn't contain the sarcasm that filtered through my voice.

"And you're with Carlos now? You always had the hots for him."

I stalled for time. "I don't know what you mean."

"I knew you were messing with him before we filed for divorce. The goddamn city knew."

"We won't revisit the affairs you had." There was only so much I could take.

"I was just too much of a gentleman to embarrass the mother of my children. You can hardly blame me for our marriage failing."

"I thought you called to check how I am?" I said. "But since we're talking, I want you to know that I plan to take the kids with me for a vacation in Karachi. I believe I'll need a notarized letter from you." The idea of spending summer vacation in Karachi and visiting the mountains had percolated within me since I had returned to Houston, but I had not articulated my desire to anyone, not even Amman. I kicked myself for telling Jim—especially during a heated moment—and not waiting until I had worked out a plan.

Jim's response was not a surprise. "We'll see. I don't think I can let my children leave the country to spend time in the hotbed of terrorism and drugs."

"'Hotbed of terrorism? Drugs?' We'll discuss later! I need to rest now." My hands shook when I set the phone down. Consoling myself with a reminder that I had six months to make my plan work, I closed my eyes and tried to take a nap.

*　*　*

I relaxed on the sofa, watching Amman pour milk into the children's cereal bowls. Winter break had ended, and Amman had extended her stay since I needed another week before I could resume work. She helped the children pack their school bags and walked them to the bus, chatting with them as if she had known her grandchildren their entire lives.

But while the outside world reverted to order, I was conscious of my mind filled with images from dreams in which Amman tried to sweep crumpled bits of paper, and how every time she tried to gather the paper up, a gust of wind swirled the pile away from her.

I knew what I wanted to ask her. I sipped my tea and watched her as she floated between the rooms, humming a Lata Mangeshkar film song from long ago. She picked up VCR tapes, stacked children's books, and put away sneakers that were strewn around the room.

Finished with her tasks, she went upstairs and returned with a package. "Years ago, I bought this for Jim when I was in Delhi," she said, unfolding a white silk kurta. "Do you think this might fit Carlos? Or maybe you could save it for Sam?"

I took a sip of tea. She had undergone transformation: She accepted Carlos, or perhaps she always had, and I hadn't noticed. She was also making an effort to refer to Sam by his nickname. "I can see if Carlos likes it."

Amman refolded the shirt and handed it to me. "I'll leave it here so you can give it to him."

"I'm sure he'll appreciate it. Thank you for accepting him."

She headed for the door. "Baita, this is your life. You have the right to choose your relationships."

She left the room with her face flushed. Minutes later, sounds of clanking pots, running water, and sizzling onions thrown into heated oil followed by the smell of turmeric and crushed coriander burst out from the kitchen. Ever since Amman had arrived, every meal she cooked saturated the house's walls with spices that I had almost forgotten. While I was away, Janet had driven Amman to the Hillcroft neighborhood where Amman bought cardamom, cumin, and curry leaves. The kids had taken a liking to the food that she prepared, and I enjoyed every bite.

Like a cat getting ready to pounce, I read the paper, remaining alert to Amman's movements. I had waited years to have this conversation with her, so a few days here or there did not matter.

Around noon as I awakened from my nap, Amman entered the study with a pot of tea, leaving cooked vegetables and daal on the stove. "Lunch will be ready soon. Such a pretty day outside! Perhaps we can go for a stroll if you feel strong?"

I nodded. "Good idea." The sun was bright and temperatures had dropped. "Amman, I'm glad you tell stories to the children. I'm sorry I was upset earlier..."

Her needles flashed steel in the afternoon sun.

I swallowed. "I have to ask you. Where did you go that night?"

Amman's needles slowed down.

"You and Abu had a fight. You would have left him—if I hadn't been sick. You went out, but you didn't go to see Heera."

Amman put her knitting on her lap. "Baita, everything that you ask me today could have been told years ago. Each time I hear your... brother's name, tears well up in my eyes. He could listen to the wind and gather stories. He knew how to listen. Often, I was lonely, and I talked to your twin. But you, Baita, you were busy with your parrots, dogs, and cats." The creases in her forehead seemed to have been wiped away. "Baita—I've waited many years to talk to you."

fourteen

LAILA

Yasmeen sits on her sofa, wrapped up in a blanket, and I have a clear view of her face. My daughter. I have waited a long time for this moment.

"You're right. I wasn't with Heera—as I said I was that night. In order for you to understand my situation, I'll have to begin this story from before you were born. Are you able to sit through that?"

Yasmeen nods.

*   *   *

During the summer of 1952, Heera was admitted in the Abbottabad hospital for surgery, so the damage from her polio could be addressed. She and I must have been ten years old. My mother took me to the hospital to see her, but when I found her bed, she wasn't there. Instead, a boy who was about our age, sat by her bedside, reading a Munshi Prem Chand book. Through talking to him, I learned that he was Heera's doctor's son and that Heera was exercising her leg. This is the way in which my friendship with this man... boy... began. We chatted as we waited for Heera. He told me that when he grew up, he wanted to build bridges and water reservoirs. Partition had taken place only a decade ago, and Pakistan was a young country. There was hope and much work needed to be done. He loved to talk about his desire to study engineering.

"We have so many resources in the north," he would tell me. "When I grow up, I'll make sure they're not wasted."

Heera had not considered getting an education, but listening to my friend and me, she also decided that she would go to college.

"We have to do something for our country," we would say to each other. "We have to get education!"

Our new friend said, "If you don't educate yourself, you'll get married and your husbands won't have respect for you!"

During our conversations by Heera's hospital bed, I resolved to make sure that I obtained a degree in art after which I would teach as other women in my family had done. And Heera promised to resume school, so she could pass her Matric exam to enter college.

The next few summers whenever I went to Hawagali, I got news of our... friend... through Heera and he sometimes visited our Hawagali house with his father. When he was seventeen, he came to 'Pindi to attend engineering college. Since our parents knew each other, he visited our home. Often, he studied with me, joined me at the park, or visited your Shireen Khala with me. She was already married. Your grandparents treated him like a family member. They never considered that one day, the two of us would wish to marry—but over time, that is what happened.

Today I think about how blind my parents had been, and I wonder how they could have permitted such closeness between him and me without realizing that our friendship would lead to the inevitable. Perhaps they thought that no one from our Muhajir background could feel that way toward someone from the north, a Pathan. We remained connected to our family roots in India and spoke Urdu while his family communicated in Pushto. There were other differences. We came from an urban background, while his family lived and worked in the mountains. My parents trusted that while he and I could be friends, we would not cross the lines that divided us. They were wrong.

By the time I turned twenty-two, I received an engagement proposal from your father's family. My parents agreed on my behalf, but I went on a hunger strike. My friend's mother visited our 'Pindi home with a marriage proposal, and even though I wanted to accept, she was turned away. The year was 1964, before our second war with India. People were infused with nationalism—and my engineer friend had sent me letters saying that he was planning to enlist in the army.

That terrified me. I also knew that my family would never accept the man I loved. In the meantime, our family business was reeling. Your father promised to help us. Everyone pressured me, and I could not refuse any longer. In the madness of the moment, I gave in to pressure and married your father.

After you and Yasir were born, I used to receive news of... *him* through Heera when she wrote me, or when I saw her in Hawagali where she had begun teaching. She told me that our friend had moved to Peshawar and was working for an engineering company, as he had dreamed of when he was younger. He remained unmarried, she told me.

By then, your father's cotton factories had expanded. He and I traveled a good deal, and I was getting to see the world. Even though your father got angry sometimes, he cared for me. And I loved you and Yasir too much to think of leaving him. When my thoughts strayed to my friend, I smiled at my teenage foolishness.

One summer, when we were in Hawagali, Heera mentioned that my friend planned to visit Hawagali and that she was going to see him. That week, I remained in the house to avoid running into him. But one afternoon, I decided to walk with you and your brother to the park. I saw him on the street. Once the awkwardness wore off, we started talking about 'Pindi, and about our college days. In many ways, he was the same friend that I had met when I was ten years old. But he had undergone change. He had lines on his face. His parents had passed away and one of his brothers had been killed in the 1971 war.

After I saw him, I talked to Heera about the coincidence of his reappearance at a time when I had been contemplating leaving your father. The next day, he met me in Titlipark. We sat on a bench and talked till nighttime fell. He told me that he had never stopped thinking of me, and that his love for me was the reason he had never married. I reminded him that I had children and that I couldn't leave my marriage. He understood and said that he wanted to be my friend.

But as your father's temper erupted and our marriage deteriorated, my friend became concerned for my well-being. I also was afraid that your father would learn about my renewed friendship and that he would misconstrue it. Once, when your father was in Hawagali for a brief stay, he got angry with me. He said that I had cooked the wrong meal—or something small like that. But really, he was angry because

Pakistan was in turmoil. His factories had been nationalized under Bhutto, and then General Zia had declared a coup. In his contentious mood, your father was looking to fight. He pushed me across the room. I fell on my arm, nearly breaking it. The next morning your father left for 'Pindi and onward to Karachi.

*　　*　　*

I take a sip of water, close my eyes, and relive that day all over again, as I have countless times before. Yasmeen's eyes are pinned on me. I lose myself in my thoughts.

*　　*　　*

Early morning, when Tariq's car turns the corner and smoke from his car's silencer dissolves in the mountain air, I inform the ayah that I am going to see Heera. I leave my car outside Heera's house and walk to the cottage where Athar stays. Sleep in his eyes and dressed only in a vest and a shalwar, Athar opens the door. Seeing my cradled arm, he hurries me inside. I smell sleep on his body.

Depositing me on a chair, he asks to see my arm. "I'm a doctor's son, remember?"

I roll up my sleeve, allowing Athar to press the swelling on my arm. I wince.

"You should get it seen by a doctor," Athar says when he returns with a cloth that he begins to wind around my arm. "It's not broken, but it could have been." He stands up and punches the cupboard door shut. His face remains unchanged, but his knuckles are red. "That bastard. He can't get away with this."

He paces the room, and I realize that this is the first time I have entered Athar's borrowed cottage—a bachelor's bungalow with a living room, an adjoining kitchen, and a bedroom. An open door reveals a bed with rumpled sheets. When I look up at Athar, the dark suns of his eyes burn into mine.

My breath becomes shallow, but I remain in my chair. In two strides, Athar is beside me. Our bodies clinging together, we stumble onto his bed.

*   *   *

I open my eyes, struggling to find words to share my story with Yasmeen. Never have I discussed with her the intimacy between men and women. Times may have changed, but when I was raising Yasmeen, mothers left their daughters to learn about relationships on their own wedding nights. And here I am, telling my daughter some of my deepest secrets, struggling to utter his name out loud.

I expel a breath. "My... friend and I... we became... lovers the morning after your father nearly broke my arm."

I sit down and pick up the story from where I left off:

*   *   *

Afterwards, we felt remorse for our action, but we couldn't erase what we had done. And once we crossed the line, we could not turn back. He begged me to leave your father, but I was afraid. You two were young, and I couldn't leave you. General Zia had passed Shariah anti-adultery laws—remember? The world around us had gone mad. Americans had flooded our streets with weapons, Afghans had poured into the country, and Zia had enforced extremist laws against women and minorities. I could not conceive leaving your father. Having this relationship was terrifying. Yet, we could not stop.

After that morning I began visiting my friend's cottage. Closeness with him was my only opportunity to be happy. Sometimes, after being with him I would return to our house, pick up the Dawn newspaper and read about a man and woman getting publicly lashed because their families opposed their romantic relationship, or I would read about a woman being found guilty after reporting a rape—Zia had passed a law where women's words equaled half that of a man's. I would sit with you children, feed you dinner, and think how much I loved you but I'd also think of my love for him. Though I knew such punishments would not be doled out to those with privilege, I also was aware of risk. But I could not stop.

By the second summer of this secrecy, I had a routine. I took the car, telling everyone in the house that I was going to visit Heera. I would park the car outside Heera's house and cover myself under a chaddar. Today it's so strange to think of me donning so much cloth to hide myself—you know I never liked women to be covered, but this was one time in my life when I used a religious cover to disguise myself.

Back then, Hawagali was not so built up, so my activities went unnoticed. He came up to Hawagali for a few days at a time, but often enough so we could meet. At first, I didn't think the affair would last long. As time went by, he and I wanted to be with each other. Only the thought of you two—my children—kept me in my marriage.

Sometimes, I felt guilty about deceiving your father, but my feelings for him were too strong to contain. By the time you children were sixteen, I was seeing him at least three times a week every summer except for when your father was there.

The year you and Yasir turned seventeen was a turning point. My... friend's family was pressuring him to marry a woman they had selected for him. And he no longer had any excuses. He gave in and met her. He told me that he liked the woman. She was educated and attractive, and he wanted to start his own family. He issued me an ultimatum. "Either you leave your husband," he told me. "Or I'll marry someone."

His demand was not a surprise to me. The secrecy of our relationship was wearing us down. We had been meeting for almost four years. The outside world had become even worse: Zia remained in power, refugees, guns, and heroin continued to pour in, and religious fanaticism was on the rise. I knew that I had run out of time. He no longer wanted to live in Pakistan.

He was aware of my fear that your father would not grant me divorce. So he offered me a solution. "We can leave Pakistan," he said. "We can go to New Zealand and begin a new life there."

He told me that his brother in Auckland had promised him a job with an engineering company and had invited him to bring me and you children if I wanted.

*　　*　　*

I pause and walk to the window in Yasmeen's study. A gust blows outside, bending the Chinese tallow tree low, shaking yellow leaves to the ground. I lean my cheek against the glass window.

*　　*　　*

118

"We can live a new life!" He takes my hands in his.

I break away from him and apply my lipstick, focusing on the rose-patterned wallpaper I know too well. Athar plucks my lipstick out of my hands and interjects his frame between me and the mirror. He wears a vest and a shalwar, its folds bunched up in his waist. I allow him to hold me close.

"We can invite your children to join us in our new life," he says. "They're old enough to attend university in New Zealand. Our lives are slipping away. I have given so much to this land. For what? We have a war on our borders. The army runs our land. Everything I dreamed of has slipped away. There's no freedom for people like us. Why stay here? Leave with me."

I stand up and press myself against his body, a terrain I know well after four forbidden years. His eyes have deeper lines around the edges. My face is also older, and my shoulders slump. Living a double life is catching up on us.

"Let's leave this hell-hole," he urges. "We have to live our lives. You and I belong together. I am your Qais and I will go mad without you."

He and I have joked about the Laila Majnoon folk-tale many times. In the story, Qais falls in love with Laila and loses his mind because he is not permitted to unite with his love. We cannot wait any longer. Either I leave with him, or our lives together have to end. The bedroom where we meet feels like a cupboard box. Even the rose-patterned wallpaper is faded.

*   *   *

Yasmeen sits on the sofa, watching my face.
I sit down and continue the story:

*   *   *

That afternoon, I agreed to leave Pakistan with him. Throwing off my chaddar's restrictive cover so I could feel the sun on my arms and see the daisies without the shadow of a covering, I walked to Heera's house. I could not live a double life any longer. I dreamt about the future when *he* and I could walk in the sunshine together—in another country—without hiding. I wanted Yasir to study music and poetry as

119

he had always yearned without pressure from your father. I wanted freedom for myself.

He and I fixed a date for me to bring you and Yasir to 'Pindi—he would follow in his own car—and on the drive, I planned to tell you everything. When we reached 'Pindi, I would introduce you to him.

However, as you remember, qismat was not on our side. Without warning, your father drove to Hawagali the day before our planned departure. You contracted a fever. I paced in your room, writing *him* a note to tell him that I couldn't leave without both of you—that's the paper you remember in your room. I first thought I would send my note through the chowkidar, but I felt unsafe. Fortunately, your fever subsided. I threw away the paper and drove to his cottage. That night, I didn't bother with a chaddar for I knew that the deception would end soon.

*　　*　　*

I halt. "The rest you know. I went out that night. Yasir went to look for me. I was with him. When I returned, our lives changed forever."

Yasmeen wraps her blanket around her body. "I don't understand. Why didn't you leave with... your... friend later? What was his name, Amman?"

I bend to pick up a tuft of cat-hair. "His name was Athar." The room feels cold. I have not uttered his name for a long time.

"I wanted to go to New Zealand after Yasir's accident. But your father had a heart attack. I kept telling my friend to wait for me, that I would leave soon, and that you and I would join him. You began sleepwalking. I was afraid for you. What if your sleepwalking got worse, and you ended up hurting yourself, or what if your father had another more severe heart attack? I would have even more weighing on my conscience than I already did.

"My... friend waited a full year after the accident, communicating with me through Heera. Finally, he gave up and flew to New Zealand to join his brother. Perhaps if he had waited longer, I would have gone with him. I don't know. We dropped out of touch... and I have not heard from him since."

Yasmeen pulls the comforter closer to her chest. I slump in the sofa feeling as if someone has pulled a dark rope from inside my belly out of my throat. And now the rope, a dark snake, lies uncoiled on Yasmeen's study floor.

fifteen

YASMEEN

The front door clicked shut as Amman stepped outside to go for a walk. I lay with my chin rooted in my palms and stared at my fingernails. Too short. One day, I would grow them long. I bit into a cuticle and tasted blood.

A snort escaped my nose. Amman just told me about her affair, and the truth about what happened on the night that Yasir passed away, and I was worrying about my cuticles.

* * *

Our horsewallah, Javed Khan, a tall, straight-backed man, ambles to our house with his horses. "Sahib, today is perfect for a ride." He taps his stick on the ground, soft from the rain.

Yasir lies under a fir tree, a blade of grass in his mouth, wishing he could exchange it for a cigarette, but he cannot smoke in full view of the house. Even though he's a known rebel, he adheres to our family norm where teenagers don't light up in front of adult family members. Relishing the freedom of mountain life, Yasir jumps to his feet. "Let's go, Yas."

I clamber on a horse. Riding with Yasir is fun, even if this year—for the first time—he and I argue about the new neighbors with whom he smokes charas-pot.

We canter along roads that are deserted except for occasional strollers. When we reach the trail-head, Yasir and Javed Khan veer upwards. I yank my rein to urge my horse, Masoom, to follow them, but she halts, more interested in grazing by the roadside. I dig my heels into her side, but she tosses her mane and continues eating roadside grass. I remain seated, waiting for her to finish.

Yasir's voice wafts down the hillside. "Coming, Yas?"

I pull at Masoom's reins and dig my spurs again.

"Need help?" A man's voice speaks up from behind me.

I turn around to see a tall man with deep eyes and hair wavier than Yasir's standing behind me. He pins his eyes on me and nods as if he knows me from somewhere.

Embarrassed by his gaze, I turn my face away. "I'm fine." I wish Masoom would hurry up so I can move on.

The man approaches Masoom and strokes her neck. She neighs at his touch. "Never let the horse eat while you are on her," he says. "If she's hungry, you can get off and let her eat. But normally horses can wait. When you reach your destination, you can let her eat."

I gulp, wishing I could recognize the man who is knowledgeable about horses and interested in talking to me. The sensation that we had met earlier lingers. Though I recognize the timbre of his voice, I cannot place him.

"Be firm. You can be tough and gentle at the same time." As soon as he tugs at Masoom's reins, she stops eating and is ready to ascend the mountainside. "See? And don't pull so hard that the bit cuts her mouth."

He reaches into his pocket and draws out a brown paper bag, which he offers me. "This is for when you reach your destination—for you and the horse."

Smelling fresh peanuts, I accept the bag from him. Masoom snorts.

"Remember—firm, not cruel with that rein."

We hear horse hooves pound on the trail above me—Yasir has returned to check on my whereabouts.

"Goodbye," the man says. He walks away as if the encounter extended longer than he intended.

Yasir reaches me as the man turns the corner. "You know we're not supposed to talk to strangers." He mimics Amman's voice. "Who was that?"

"Some man. He gave me peanuts." I tug Masoom's reins in the way that the stranger demonstrated. Masoom obeys. "He acted as if he knew me. I thought he was going to say my name."

"Maybe he's some acquaintance of Amman's. Everyone knows her."

We arrive at Titlipark, the highest point in Hawagali, and flop on purple heather where Yasir and Javed Khan light up their cigarettes. Masoom and I munch on peanuts. I ask Javed Khan if he knew who the tall man was.

"No Bibi," he replies. "He must be here for the day only. Many city folk drive north for shorter visits."

Later that afternoon I mean to ask Amman if she knows the man with the peanuts, but she doesn't return till late evening, and I forget my question.

*   *   *

I traced my hand along my cat Horace's fur, enjoying his coffee-grinder purr on my belly. My anger toward Amman slipped away like an ice cube on a sweaty face. I could not be angry with Amman for doing what I had done with Carlos. No wonder the man had gazed at me in such a familiar manner. His attentiveness toward me was similar to the way Carlos watched and treated my children. Every time Sam and Saira spoke or laughed, Carlos looked at me. Later, he gave me his assessment: "Your son's eyes are like yours," or "Saira's laughter seems to come from her dad."

I was only fifteen the summer when I met Amman's lover by the roadside. Amman must have stayed with him for another few years after that encounter. The man knew who I was even though my frame was smaller than Amman's; my smile made me her daughter.

*   *   *

Wind raced against my face, reddening my cheeks. I held out my arms to embrace the air like I used to when my father took us for drives to Clifton and Seaview.

Carlos glanced at me. "Sure you're not cold?"

I shook my head and leaned into the wind. Memorial Park's trail was quiet. Through the pine trees, I could see the freeway also drained of cars. January was a quiet month in Houston, with trees stripped of foliage and residents away for breaks.

We walked along the gravelly path, holding hands, past the warm-up area where a man in a tank top undertook pushups on a bench. The air was humid, but sun rays filtered through clouds. We sat on a bench, our backs to the netted golf course behind us.

I shared Amman's story with Carlos. When I finished, he let out a low whistle, flicking his fingers as if his tips were burning. "That's some tale. Your mom. Who'd have guessed?" He shook his head so fast that it looked as if it would wobble off his shoulders.

I closed my eyes.

"They certainly took a risk."

"Affairs are fairly common amidst a certain class of people."

"And your father? He passed away without knowing?"

I stared at the city skyline. "I think we all suspected. Including my father. I'm sure that's what their fight was about... the night my... twin..."

*　　*　　*

Yasir and I notice Amman's behavior during the summer when we meet the tall man, but we fail to connect the two occurrences. One rainy afternoon in Hawagali, I lie in my room reading.

Yasir sprawls on the sofa, his legs stretching over the edge. "I'm worried about Amman," he says. "She's been acting strange. You noticed? She drives off by herself with her sketch-pad. She wants to be alone all the time. I even heard her say to Shireen Khala that she didn't want her to come visit us this summer." Yasir's curly hair waves like insect feelers.

Walking to the window, I gaze at the spot where Amman's car should be parked.

Over dinner that evening when we ask her if she's okay, she responds: "I'm practicing drawing."

The next morning, I watch her brush powder on her cheeks. She uses a different puff to powder her back. I wonder why she's getting dressed up to go drawing.

She heads for the door, calling "I'll be at Heera's! And then I'll go sketching."

Sitting in the trail of her jasmine oil, I am aware, just as everyone else is. But no one says anything. Amman goes out for six hours. She returns and walks to her room, sketchbook tucked under her arm. When she emerges, bathed and refreshed for dinner, she has no drawings to show. In Karachi, she gets around in a car with a driver, but in the mountains, where roads are more dangerous because of mist and curves, Amman drives without any worries. And we never question her movement.

"Can we see?" Yasir asks.

She shakes her head. "I'm out of practice. I'll show you when my work improves." But she never does. Instead, she moves around the house, dusting cabinets, instructing the cook, singing and humming. Sometimes she returns past dusk, her hair disheveled as if blown by the breeze, a smile settled on her lips. Yasir and I wonder what she has been drawing in the dark.

*   *   *

Carlos tossed a pinecone in the air. "I don't understand how your mom kept her secret. That place sounds small. No one saw her?"

"I guess not." Houston's landscape with its pine trees was different from Hawagali, where pine trees leaned into the hills and snow-clad mountain peaks obstructed views of the sky. Houston was flat, and no matter how high fir trees tips stretched, blue sky remained visible.

"Quite a story."

I sighed. "I don't know what I was angry about all these years. That Amman should have left and made her life with her lover? That my twin passed away even as my mother tried to deal with her life? Twenty years later, it's weird to hear her talk about her... lover. In typical Pakistani fashion, she can't say his first name, referring to him as 'my friend' or just simply him. She can be so old-fashioned and then be so racy. And no one confronted her."

"You can't talk about being old-fashioned. Didn't you marry Jim because you got knocked up? And that was here, in the wonderful US of A."

I winced. "You don't have to bring that up."

"You did say no one confronted your mom."

I scuffed my sneaker into dirt. "Point taken. Did I tell you that my mother is named after a heroine in a popular folk-tale?"

"You can change the subject."

I laughed. "I'm going to. The story is a bit like Romeo and Juliet. A poet called Qais falls in love with a woman, but they cannot marry. He writes love poetry and people refer to him as Majnoon, which means madman. There are many versions of the tragedy—but each one ends with death."

* * *

Amman was cleaning the kitchen when I returned to the house. I stood behind her and watched her arm circle the sponge over the countertop. Her loose hair cascaded down her back. She must have just washed it. I wanted to smooth her furrowed forehead, but my arms seemed glued to my side.

"Are you ready for lunch?" she asked.

I felt my tongue stuck in my mouth as if I had to scrape for words in a language that I was learning. My family told spell-binding stories, but we could never gather up words when we had to connect with each other. "I'm sorry I was so angry..."

She kissed my cheek. "It's okay." She sat down and poured tea for both of us.

A wintry wind blasted through the kitchen window. After closing the glass, I joined Amman at the kitchen table. Sugar granules were spilled on the wooden surface. With my fingers, I pushed them in a heap. I didn't have to look at Amman to know that we remembered the same image.

* * *

Soaking wet and blinded by the rain, Yasir limps down the road. Delirious with fever, I sense the danger he faces, but I am in my bedroom and I cannot help him. Abu paces in his room. Outside, rain rages.

Abu stops by my room, his footfall thudding on the wood floor. "Where's Yasir?" he asks.

"Gone to look for Amman," I say.

He leaves the room. The front door slams and I hear his car engine roar. After the sound of rain, I hear Abu's car engine again. He's back from his search. Plastic rustles as Abu puts on his raincoat and snaps open his umbrella. His stick taps against the front door. Through the rain, I hear him calling for the gatekeeper. Why is he coming and going, and where is Yasir? I hear the gatekeeper and Abu leaving the house together.

In my mind's eye, I see Yasir struggle to get up, but he has lost strength. His body is soaked. His head lies on golden pine needles. He sleeps amidst a clump of cobra plants where Abu and the chowkidar find him. They ask the villagers for a tonga-horse carriage to bring him to the house. The gatekeeper runs for the village doctor.

I cannot wait in my bed any longer. I know they are bringing Yasir home. Amman, a splash of blue paint with mist in her eyes, returns from her lover's arms to find me on the stairs, teeth chattering with cold. She hurries me to bed. I lie back, aware of the horse carriage carrying Yasir's body.

I lift my head and try to tell her what happened, but no words leave my parched throat. From my bed, my eyes closed, I see the carriage approaching. Amman rushes out to meet Abu. The pictures turn hazy. Like Yasir, I lose consciousness and fall into darkness.

Yasir leaves us early in the morning. Afterwards, the doctor pumps tranquilizers into my system. Despite the medicine, I dream about swooping kaneezes, swirling Yasir, mocking him, covering him with layers of black cloth. High above, crows shriek, their yellow eyes shining in the moonlight. The ground is alive with swirling cobra plants.

The next morning, I awaken with a vision of Yasir beneath white cloth. I know he has left us.

And in the bright sunshine, my eye falls on a crumpled ball of paper in the corner that appears as large as Nanga Parbat, the snow-capped mountain peak that we see from the park on clear days. I leap out of bed and grab the unsent note, not noticing Amman entering the room.

In two strides, she reaches me, extricates the wad from my grasp and tosses the paper into the fireplace's dying embers. A spurt of red flame tears into the paper, leaving transparent film that crumbles into ashes.

BOOK TWO

sixteen

YASMEEN

I leaned my head against the airplane window. Beside me, Sam was stretched out on two seats with his head on my lap. Across the aisle, Saira lay asleep on three seats.

So many years since I had flown the twenty-four hour trans-Atlantic—no, trans-world—journey from the US to Pakistan. Though I had spent time in Europe with Jim, I had not stopped at airports that connected flights from the Middle East to South Asia. Now, during the few hours of our Dubai stopover, a line of South Asian passengers—men, women, and children—rested against hand luggage handles, resigned to four-hour waits as their papers were scrutinized. A Pakistani woman had been pulled out of line. She sat on her haunches staring at her hand luggage, while her children hovered behind her, their hands on her shoulders. Her husband was probably being strip-searched somewhere in the terminal.

Our western appearance seemed to separate my children and me from scrutiny, but I wondered how we would be treated in Karachi with our "foreign" passports. I was grateful yet again that the journey was long. I needed time to transition from our Houston schedules to Karachi's traffic and the barrage of relatives.

Sam stretched his arms. "Will we get burgers and French fries?"

I clicked my tongue. This was Jim's doing. I never offered fast food to the children. "Food will be different in Karachi. You'll have to be patient and not grumble. It'll make Nani upset."

Sam widened his eyes: "Like how different?"

"You'll get western food." Sam had asked me this question several times before we even boarded the flight in Houston. Clearly, the children had heard their father's explosions when I first informed him that I wanted to take the children for the summer—and maybe longer—to spend time with Amman in Karachi.

*   *   *

One afternoon when I pick up the children from school, Saira's face is streaked with tears. Leaving the car double-parked with its engine running—something I never do because I'm so paranoid about things being stolen before my eyes—I jump out to hug my daughter.

The moment we drive away from school, Sam says, "Mom, these boys, they pushed her. And she fell down."

I pull the car into the parking of a shopping strip along Buffalo Speedway. Holding Saira's hand, I ask her to tell me what happened. She shakes her head.

"They told her to go away," Sam answers for his sister. "And they called her mean words. This one boy pretend-shot her. And then his mom came and got him. I'll take them on tomorrow. I promise."

The next day, instead of walking Saira and Sam to the bus, I take the day off and drive to Galveston where the children and I collect seashells and splash in the water. The children rarely miss school, but the school-year is about to end, and I need a day to cool down before I talk to the principal again.

That evening, after tucking the children to bed, I call Jim and tell him that I plan to take the children with me to spend the summer in Karachi. "They need to meet their family," I tell him. "And they need to get away."

"What do you mean 'their' family?" he says. "That's not safe. I'm going to get a lawyer on this one."

I hold the phone away from my ear and let him rant. I know he won't be able to stop me. I'm their mother. Plus, through mutual friends, I know that his new partner doesn't want children around.

After we hang up, I walk toward my window and inhale the fragrance from star jasmine that has begun to blossom from the vine below. I close my eyes and try to recall Jim from when we met in

132

college. Eager to learn about South Asia, he presented me with daily questions about my home city: "What's a landmark that you love?" or "Describe a sound that you associate with the space," or "Name your favorite restaurant and the scent of the dish you loved most."

But our relationship had changed. I had to schedule a meeting with our lawyers in order to gain his signature on a notarized letter permitting me to leave the US with our children. He almost refused to sign, but caved in when I reminded him of the questions he used to ask about Karachi. I also agreed to sign a contract pledging to bring the children back to Houston before the start of the academic year.

*　　*　　*

The pilot's voice buzzed over the microphones, informing passengers that the airplane would soon land in Karachi. From the window, we saw the city sparkling below us, stretching miles into the desert. On the other side of the lights was the Arabian Sea over which we had just flown.

As we collected our belongings, a bearded man across the aisle fixed his gaze at my sweater and jeans, his disapproval a reminder of what was to come: a country facing growing extremism, a backlash against General Musharraf's alignment with the US, and the post-9/11 US bombings in Afghanistan. I returned the man's stare until his eyes slid away.

Ahead of us, a German couple strapped on their backpacks. I wondered if they were flying through Karachi on their way to Nepal. No other western tourists were on the airplane. Tourism in Pakistan had ended after 9/11. The rest of the passengers around us were Pakistani businessmen, mothers with children, college students returning home for the summer, and laborers returning from the Middle East; United States' State Department warnings never deterred Pakistani families from returning home.

Wheeling our hand-luggage, the children and I walked through the chute that connected the airplane to the terminal. The last time that I had been in Karachi airport before flying off to college, passengers had to ride buses and climb stairs to board. Modernization had hit Karachi, and I had missed the transition. The terminal, lit by neon lights, was deserted except for security guards who stood as straight as the rifles strapped to their sides.

The immigration line for Pakistani citizens was long, packed with working class men returning from Dubai or Saudi Arabia, while the line marked for "non-Pakistanis" moved faster. Nearly twenty years ago, when I had flown out of Karachi on a Lufthansa flight—an airline that no longer flew through Karachi because of hijackings—I did not know that I would return using a US passport stamped with a visitor's visa.

The baggage terminal area had also been modernized. I noted signs for restrooms, drinking fountains, and pay phones. After clearing customs, we hired a porter who wheeled the trolley through the open glass exit, guarded by more armed security. Beneath the shaded area, hundreds of bodies waited to greet family members who would be arriving from Dubai armed with televisions and VCRs.

The children had never seen so many humans compressed together, and they stayed close to me. Moisture, heat, and the smell of perspiration blasted our senses, even though the sun had risen only an hour earlier. Karachi airport was busiest through the night and early morning when international flights landed or left the city.

"Taxi, Memsahib?"

"Guide, Madam?"

"Assistance, Miss?"

Blinded by the heat and voices, I searched for Amman's tall figure.

A uniformed man pushed the taxi drivers away. "Let Memsahib pass."

I nodded thanks to him, and he was by my side. "Madam, you need hotel?"

"Yasmeen!" Amman was to my left. When Amman had insisted that she would meet us at the airport I had tried to dissuade her, but I had forgotten the avalanche of bodies at the airport.

With the porter behind me and the children attached to me, I pushed past the crowd to reach Amman. A medium sized man in his early twenties stood beside her. She introduced him to us as Akram, the son of our driver who had dropped me off years ago. As we waited for Akram to bring the car closer, my eyes fell on another change that had evolved during my eighteen-year absence. In front of the airport sat an American fast-food burger chain, emitting grease and smoke.

The multi-lane Shara-e Faisal was clogged with buses, motor-cycles, and taxis. In the divider, lignum and neem trees struggled to survive desert heat. Streets were filled with men carrying briefcases, running to catch buses, while others held hands and walked toward tea canteens. City sweepers bent low, swinging twig brooms as they attempted to collect dirt and garbage, and mothers walked uniformed children to schools. If we drove along a side street, we would be sure to catch sight of men crouched low, pissing against yellow walls.

A motorcyclist threaded between diesel fumes emitted by buses and trucks while his wife sat sideways behind him, holding their daughter between them. A second child sat on the handlebars. Buses were decorated with truck art mirrors, glassy designs, and paintings while men hung out of bus doors or sat on luggage racks. A Suzuki van passed us. I laughed when I saw its sign that read "honk please" in Urdu and in English. When Akram blew his horn, the van driver flapped his hand so Akram could pass him. Most sights and sounds were the same as before, but I noted subtle differences. Billboards advertised cars, US fast food chains, and designer shalwar kameezes—none of which had been visible during the Zia era.

Amman interrupted my thoughts: "Uncle Sikandar might drop in for tea. I hope that's okay?"

I nodded. The last time that I had seen Amman's eldest brother was when he visited New York for a conference, and Jim and I had driven from Boston to meet him. He returned to Karachi with a positive review of Jim.

In our driveway, the first sound that I heard was the whistle of a koel, a bird that beckoned the arrival of summer and mango season. The koel's song was echoed by the guttural cooing of pigeons squatting on the roof. I exhaled. With or without Yasir, early morning in Karachi was the same.

seventeen

LAILA

The children yawn over the no-spice dinner that I prepared for them.

"I don't want you getting sick," I tell them as I ladle potatoes onto Saira's plate. "We'll wait a few days before you eat spicy food." From the experience of other visitors from abroad, I know that the children will experience at least one bout of diarrhea before their systems stabilize.

Yasmeen rests her chin on her palm to watch me fuss over my grandchildren before escorting them to bed. When I enter the children's bedroom—Yasmeen's childhood room—I find her lying beside her son. She does not look up as I enter and walk toward a bureau to open and close drawers. My daughter understands that I am in the room because I want to be close to her and my grandchildren. She and Sameer are cramped on the twin bed, the one in which she slept when she was his age. During the shuffle of Yasmeen and Yasir's youth, new beds were never purchased, even after Yasir's body outgrew the length of his bed, as if he were not meant to get older.

"Mom! I'm not sleepy. Can we call Dad?" Sameer sits up and rubs his eyes.

Yasmeen's response is more patient than I expect. "This is not a good time to call Houston. It's too early in the morning. You can call him when you wake up tomorrow."

Saira's eyes are fixed on the curtains that flutter beside the air-conditioning unit; few Karachi homes have central air-conditioning. Although I am happy that Yasmeen is in Karachi with her children, I'm aware of how difficult this period must be for Saira. Children need time to adjust to change, and my granddaughter has experienced much turmoil over the past year.

"I want to hear a story, Mom," she says.

"A story?" Yasmeen is also tired, but she, too, is struck by her daughter's voice.

Always an opportunist, Sameer chimes in. "Come on, Mom. Something about this house."

"About this house?" Yasmeen rests her palm on her stomach. "The story I'm thinking about begins here but ends in Hawagali..."

I draw a sharp breath as Yasmeen begins:

* * *

One summer morning, Yasir and I packed our suitcases for Hawagali. We always flew to Islamabad and drove on to Hawagali, but that summer, your Nani had gone north earlier. Yasir and I begged our parents to allow us to take a train to 'Pindi. My mother agreed on the condition that one of her older cousins would ride with us—Karachi was safer in those days. Train journeys were comfortable back then and we didn't face the kind of turmoil that there is today.

Once we finished packing, I stopped by the main courtyard to bid farewell to my favorite pet, a parrot called Mithoo, who had been with us since his birth. Mithoo had a loud voice but his underdeveloped wings prevented him from flying. Most days, I walked around the house with Mithoo perched on my shoulder as he imitated sounds and voices that he picked up. The morning that we were to leave for Hawagali, Mithoo was quiet. His beady eyes looked oval and his feathers were greasy.

Yasir joined me by the cage. "Let's just take him with us," he said. "We can't leave him alone."

I smiled. The best part about having a twin was that we could read each other's minds. "What about Amman?" I said. "Won't she mind?"

Yasir flapped his hand. "She'll be fine."

At Cantt Station, our platform was packed with coolies, cold drink stalls, and families who were there to wave farewell to their relatives.

Rizwana Aunty, my mother's second cousin, waited for us outside our train car. She bustled the porter to load up our suitcases, grumbling, "What took you so long? We nearly missed the train."

The train's whistle sounded. We hurried to our cabin where the coolie deposited our bags. I placed Mithoo's covered cage on the carriage floor.

Wiping sweat from her forehead with her handkerchief, Rizwana Aunty sat down. She unscrewed her tea thermos, poured steaming liquid in her cup, and took a sip. Her eyes fell on the covered cage. She touched the cloth with her toe and asked: "What's that?" Leaning forward, she lifted the cloth to discover Mithoo in his cage. "Wha-a-a -t??"

"Wha-a-a-t?" copied Mithoo, already more energized.

I replaced the blanket. "Please don't disturb him. He needs to sleep."

"And how might we get any rest with that bird here?"

Yasir intervened. "Mithoo has to go to Hawagali with us."

Rizwana Aunty drew out a book and began to read. "I knew I shouldn't have agreed to travel with you," she spoke into her book. "This is the last time I do a favor for your parents. I hope your mother scolds you when we reach 'Pindi."

With a bag of peanuts in hand, Yasir and I climbed up to the upstairs bunk. We relaxed in the upper bunk for most of the twenty-six-hour train ride that was disrupted by occasional whistles by Mithoo, followed by threats to harm him by Rizwana Aunty.

At the 'Pindi station, Amman was on the platform to meet us. Rizwana Aunty collected her belongings and stepped out of the train toward Amman to tell her about Mithoo: "Your children are disobeying instructions," she said, certain that Amman would take her side.

* * *

Yasmeen sits up. "Do you know what your Nani said?"

"No, what?" chorused the children.

"You can ask her yourself."

I hold back my smile. Yasmeen and I are narrating a story together for the first time. "I remember that day well. Rizwana was hoping that I'd scold your mother."

"Did you?" demands Sameer.

I shake my head. "I said, 'Good thinking. I'm glad you brought Mithoo. We don't want to leave sick pets at home by themselves.' Rizwana, of course, didn't like my response."

My daughter smiles. For a passing second, a wave of fear curls in my stomach. I don't know where she will take the story. I radiated happiness that summer.

Yasmeen clears her throat and continues:

*   *   *

We said goodbye to Rizwana Khala. After a few days in Islamabad, we drove to Hawagali. When we reached our mountain home, we hung Mithoo's cage in the corridor outside my room. Within a day, Mithoo's feathers were shiny again. He crooned and sang all day, awakening us with train whistles and calls for tea, sounds that he had learned from the train ride—Mithoo was never that active in Karachi.

After a week of being in the mountains, I had a dream, which confirmed my reason for bringing Mithoo to Hawagali. In the dream, Mithoo was in Titlipark, flying so high that he was a dot in the sky. His chirping was as piercing as a peacock's call. In the dream, he swooped to rest on my shoulder.

"Thank you," he said into my ear. He soared away, somersaulting like an acrobat into the clouds.

In the morning, my twin told me that the dream ended with Mithoo starting a family in Hawagali, a part of the country that had not hosted parrots before. We were certain that our dream was a prediction that Mithoo was meant to fly.

Each day, Amman began driving us to the park for 'trial runs,' as we termed the visits. We wanted Mithoo to acclimate to the terrain and know the trees and mountains. On drives to Titlipark, Mithoo responded to our excitement, singing Sabri Brother qawwalis and American disco songs.

"What if he loves to fly so much that he never returns?" Yasir asked on our first trial run.

"Then we'll have to leave him here. And he can find us every summer. Remember our dream? He'll be here with a family when we return each summer."

Yasir and Amman agreed—they considered me the pet expert.

Flight Day arrived. We packed picnic lunches and headed toward the park. Mithoo was quiet, as if aware of the day's significance. After we finished our sandwiches, I placed Mithoo's cage on the ground. Reaching into the cage, I held his leg and placed him on the grass. I stretched out one of his wings, its entire span shorter than his body. Mithoo scratched the grass with his claw. He gazed at the sky and retreated to his cage. Yasir and I sighed.

Your Nani comforted us. "Let's leave him alone. We can keep his cage door open, so he has a choice."

We sat on a bench and began to play cards, but each time we peeked, Mithoo was still in his cage. When the sun sank behind the mountains, we packed our cards and picked up our rubbish. I was brushing off our rug when Yasir grabbed my sleeve. "Look!"

I turned around. Crooning to himself, Mithoo had stepped out of his cage to walk toward a patch of dogflowers and bluebells. We held our breath when Mithoo stretched out his left wing and then his right. He began fanning his wings. As they gathered momentum, he rose four feet into the sky. Making a circle, he descended on the grass.

Yasir gripped my arm so hard that his nails made grooves in my skin. We watched Mithoo pace the grass fast as if he were an airplane prior to take off. He flapped his wings and shot upward, making a circle above the pine trees. The scene ended like the moment in our dream with Mithoo on my shoulder. After deafening me with one of his train whistle screeches, Mithoo took off for a longer flight.

The three of us looked up until the green of Mithoo's wings dissolved into a patch of trees.

*   *   *

"Did you see him again?" demands Sameer.

Yasmeen nods. "Not that day. We waited till darkness in case he returned. When he didn't, we left birdseed and water in his bowls beneath a fir tree and drove home. Though we were glad that Mithoo could fly, we were sad. The summer slid by with us visiting Titlipark every day in the hope that we would glimpse Mithoo, but he never made an appearance. Nor did we hear his songs.

"On the last day of our visit, your Nani drove us to Titlipark. We stepped into the foggy grounds and were walking in the mist when something sharp dug into my shoulder and screeched in my ear. Mithoo! His body was a lustrous green and his wings strong and healthy as if he had been flying his entire life. I glanced at the benches where we usually picnicked and saw a smaller parrot, clearly female. Without a doubt, I knew she was Mithoo's mate and that they had found each other, the only parrots in all of Hawagali. We fed them bread crumbs and watched them fly. As far as we know, Mithoo began a parrot family in Hawagali just as our dream predicted. Maybe Mithoo and his family were the ones who chased the kaneezes out of the mountains. The last I heard there are no more kaneezes, kidnappers, or live cobra plants in Hawagali."

"And after that? Did you see him again?" Sameer asks.

"Every time we returned to Hawagali, Mithoo and his mate welcomed us. The last time that we saw him, he was with three baby parrots—his children. I haven't been back since."

"Are we going to go?" Saira speaks up for the first time. "Will they be there?"

"We will go, and we can look for Mithoo. Now go to sleep."

Yasmeen kissed the children's cheeks, I dimmed the lights, and we exited the room together.

eighteen

YASMEEN

Amman followed me through the connecting door that led into my bedroom.

Standing beneath the revolving fan, she said, "You changed the story." Her words were a comment, not a question.

I opened my suitcase and searched for my t-shirt and sweatpants. A sack of lipsticks spilled out. "Do you want any? Pick whichever colors you like. I'll give the rest to the cousins and aunts."

Amman sat down, opened the bag, and drew out a fluorescent pink. "This one's too bright for me." She uncapped a maroon one. "But this one will be lovely. These are pretty gifts, Baita. Everyone will enjoy them. You changed the story."

I unfolded my pajama top. "I had to, didn't I?" My voice was muffled as I pulled my t-shirt over my head. "I couldn't say how Athar helped."

At the mention of her ex-lover, Amman's head jerked up. She looked past the doorway.

* * *

In Hawagali, Mithoo weakens and his feathers get greasier. Every time I check his cage, I find more feathers lying on newspapers that line the cage floor. When I voice my concern to Amman, she dismisses my doubt.

143

"He'll be fine once he adjusts to the air," she says, preoccupied with combing her hair.

But the monsoons hit the mountains earlier than usual, making the air cold and damp. One morning I find Mithoo huddled in a cage corner. Six of his feathers lie on the floor, and his food and water bowls are full.

Rushing to Amman, I shout, "He's sick! He's not eating! Can't we take him to a vet in Murree? There aren't any animal doctors in Hawagali. You know that!"

"Tomorrow. I'm busy this afternoon."

I stamp my foot and return to the verandah to console Mithoo. Late afternoon, while Yasir and I race each other on Titlipark's slopes, I glimpse the tall man who helped me with my horse. Reposing on a blanket beneath a pine tree, he reads a magazine and doesn't see us. An hour later, when we round the hill, we notice the man with his blanket and magazine tucked under his arm, walking away from Amman. I ask Amman how she knows the man.

Her eyebrows leap into her hairline. "He wanted directions."

My thoughts skip to Mithoo. "I think that man knows about animals."

Amman looks up. "How do you know?"

I tell her about the time he helped me train my horse.

"If you see him during the next day or so, you can invite him to check up on Mithoo," she says, running her fingers through her hair. "And if that doesn't work, we'll drive Mithoo to Murree."

I hurl myself on the bench. "You want us to talk to a stranger?"

Amman gazes above my eye. "He seems to be from a good family. You can talk to him as long as you don't bring him inside our house. Make sure an adult is with you—the ayah or the driver."

"And what if we don't see this man? Mithoo will die!"

Amman pats my back and walks away, humming an Indian film song. "You'll see," she says over her shoulder. "Everything will work out."

The next afternoon, Yasir and I are riding the see-saw at the bowl-park near our house, complaining to each other about Amman. From the top of the see-saw, I glimpse the top of a hat, followed by a thin dark face. Yasir lowers me, and we race up the park slopes onto the road.

"Sir," I say trying to capture my breath. "Do you remember me?"

A smile breaks out on the man's face, causing a dimple to appear in his left cheek. "Of course. You're the girl on the horse. How's your riding coming along?" He takes off his hat and dips it toward me as if he is a performer bowing for applause.

"My horse listens to me now. Thank you for your help and for the peanuts. They were delicious."

Throwing his head back, the man laughs. "You can't possibly remember how the peanuts tasted one year ago! How can I serve you today? Do you need help with another horse?"

The man's smile is familiar, making my heart pound.

Yasir jumps in: "Our parrot's sick. Since you know so much about horses, we thought you might be able to help us."

The man's eyes narrow. "I'm an engineer."

I feel a prickle in my eyes. Sniffling, I hold back my tears.

The man scratches his temple. "But pets and birds seem to respond well to me. If you want, I can take a look at your parrot."

Yasir and I lead the man to our house with our ayah trailing behind us. Since Amman is nowhere in sight, we leave the man on a tree stump by the front gate. Yasir tries to search for Amman while I run upstairs to retrieve Mithoo. In the screened-in hallway where his cage sits, I find him huddled in a corner, his beak tucked inside his wing. Another feather lies on the cage floor. Yasir joins me to inform me that he can't find Amman. Deciding that she must have gone for a walk, we return outside with Mithoo's cage.

Mithoo gives a weak squawk as the man reaches his hand in and draws him out to place his ear next to Mithoo's heart. Putting Mithoo down, the man says: "Your parrot's glands are swollen—he has a cold. You need to crush his bird-seed and mix it with water. Make sure he swallows the liquid. If your parrot still cannot intake the liquid, you will need to feed him with a syringe."

With wide eyes, Yasir and I gaze at our engineer friend.

"I can tell you have a gift with animals," the man says to me. "See the way Mithoo watches you? He knows you understand him. Just be still and watch him. You'll be surprised by what you learn."

"What about my brother?" I twirl a braid of hair that has escaped my ponytail. I would rather share my abilities with my twin.

The man shakes his head. "He has other talents. But you—you have the gift of connecting with animals. Practice listening by getting still."

After our engineer friend leaves, we take Mithoo back to the verandah. I place my face on the carpet beside the cage and notice Mithoo staring into my eyes, his expression telling me he will recover. When crushing the birdseed, I reflect on our encounter and realize that we never asked the engineer his name. He seemed so familiar that the question didn't occur to us.

*   *   *

Amman handed the lipstick case back to me. "The story was more interesting in the way that you told the children."

"I didn't make up the entire narrative. Yasir and I did dream of Mithoo flying."

"And he never did, that poor parrot." Amman stood up. "Well, you had better get to sleep."

I watched her move to the door, wondering if she remembered all the segments of the story. I had to say something. "Amman, didn't you feel strange when your... friend... came to the house to see Mithoo?"

She turned around. "I don't understand your question."

"You didn't feel uncomfortable? You did ask him to help us with Mithoo, didn't you?"

"That happened a long time ago, Baita. I've told you all there's to tell." She switched topics. "Will you be ready to fly to Islamabad in a week? Your Shireen Khala wants to see you."

"Definitely. I also want to go to Hawagali..." I didn't know how to bring up the past again. Previously, in Houston, I had accused her of living in the past and not knowing how to let go. Now I was doing the same. Even though she had shared so much with me, I felt that more needed to be told. Like a cow chewing on its cud, I couldn't stop thinking about Athar, about how much he resembled Yasir and wondering if my gift of communicating with animals was passed down to me through him.

*   *   *

Returning to my house after a jog around Rice University, I share my suspicion with Carlos.

He shakes his head. "I think your mom's already told you a lot— more than most do!"

"I think... I think he and Amman... were lovers before she married Abu," I muttered, expelling a breath. "That was difficult to say!"

Carlos taps his steering wheel. "So why don't you call her and ask her?"

"She won't tell me over the phone."

He speeds down Holcombe, running a yellow light. "You won't believe her no matter what she says."

"I've booked tickets for Karachi," I tell him. "Once I get there I can ask her face to face." We are approaching my house. My neighbor's sprinkler drizzles water on his green lawn. An ache creeps into my heart, as I remember the dust and flies along Karachi roadsides. "I'm going to quit my job. When I come back, maybe I'll get certified and teach, or join a graduate program for visual art."

Carlos pulls into my driveway. "You don't think the situation in Pakistan is too dangerous?"

"The media over-sensationalizes. I'm tired of war rhetoric. When did 'terror'—an abstract noun—convert into a physical object that must be defeated?"

"I know what you mean."

I pin my eyes on the azaleas that bloom in my front yard. "I have a favor to ask. I need to focus on my trip. You and I can pick up where we left off when I get back." I want to tell him that I cannot start a new life finding resolution with the old one, but words are trapped beneath my tongue.

Carlos' forehead wrinkles. "I don't understand what you're saying..."

Carlos and I have been careful not to plan the future together, but I hear hurt in his voice. We maintain separate homes, but most evenings, he lands up at my house. "I need to focus on my trip, the children, and my family." My voice dips into my throat.

"When we were together before, we broke our relationship because of your marriage and the kids. That was understandable. But now, we're together and enjoying ourselves. Except that you're saying good-bye. Again."

"I need time. The summer. While I'm away, I need to put my Houston life on hold."

"On hold?" Carlos shakes his keys that dangle off the ignition.

"I'll come back, and we can move forward..."

Carlos' lips are set in a straight line. "You're doing what your mom did. She gave up her relationship to make everyone else happy."

I open my mouth and close it without speaking.

"You can have time—don't worry about calling or emailing me while you're away. But I can't guarantee that I'll be around on the other end. We'll take our chances. We have before." Careful not to touch me, Carlos leans forward and yanks open my door-handle.

*   *   *

Amman watched me walk over to my pink bookshelf and pick up the family photo that had rested on the top shelf from as far back as I could remember. The image focused on the four of us—Amman, Abu, Yasir, and me—standing in front of our Hawagali house, with mountain peaks in the background. Abu had his arm around Amman while Yasir held our pet dog. I felt my breath leave me. Without Abu around, I felt as if our house's living room—the space in which our parents offered bootlegged whiskey and meals to guests—had been sucked into Karachi's white sky.

During our childhood, whenever Amman flew to Islamabad to see her parents, Yasir and I experienced a softer side of our father. Abu used to take Yasir and me on drives to Playland by the beach-front, buying us all the ice-cream we could consume. Afterwards, Yasir and I ran on glistening black sand while he walked behind us, his pants rolled up to his knees. Once conflict started brewing between Abu and Yasir, I forgot how much Abu had spoiled us, especially when Amman was away.

"Amman, I'm sorry I didn't fly back after... the heart attack. I've been thinking about Abu. I miss him."

Amman's eyes were watery. "I know."

Through half-closed eyes, I glanced toward Amman. I had to ask her the question that had festered with me for months—or perhaps all my life. "Was he... our real father? Or was...?"

Amman's head jerked.

"Yasir—didn't look at all like Abu..."

Amman held up her hand to stop me. "I've told you everything."

I dropped on the bed.

"Please be more sensitive. This subject doesn't need to come up any more." Amman kissed my cheek and swept out of the room.

The house was silent. Perhaps my intuition was incorrect, but I couldn't let go of Athar's ability to connect with animals and his dimples that matched Yasir's. Nor could I forget Amman's ability to create stories, half of which were real and half were fabricated.

I sighed. Life was more complicated than I had expected. In Houston, I had thought that Amman would reveal more about her past. I hoped she would tell me that the tall man was my father, and that I had no blood connection with Abu, whom I loved and hated at the same time.

But in Pakistan, there were no straight lines, no packets with directions that explained the process step-by-step. We dropped our shoes off to the cobbler without expecting a receipt. And when the driver went to collect on our behalf, the cobbler sat on the pavement beneath a tree—always in the same place—and our shoes were returned, repaired and polished, looking new again. To participate in the system, we relied on instinct and history. But I had been away for so long that I had forgotten how to let go of directions and answers. I lay on my bed and stared at the ceiling fan.

nineteen

YASMEEN

I chewed the back of my pen and took a break from finishing my aerogram to Janet. Shouts of Saira playing hide and seek with one of the neighbors interrupted my concentration. The children were beneath the banana tree grove by the water tank, my favorite place when Yasir and I were their age. Saira's floating shriek made me smile, reminding me of long-ago afternoons at the house. The ease with which the kids had adjusted to Karachi life—where their only exit out of the house was in a car—surprised me. Perhaps they found the shift to Karachi easier because life was opposite to the way they lived in Houston.

The afternoon prayer call tumbled through a nearby mosque's loudspeaker, drowning out the children's voices. A few streets away was the Bhutto home, sealed off and guarded by soldiers behind sandbags. The ex-prime minister had been executed by General Zia; his daughter had been elected, deposed, and she was again in exile. A horn blared, followed by footsteps along the corridor. My cousin Fazila had arrived to take Saira and me shopping.

Fazila tapped on my doorway, pushed the curtains open to enter and kiss me on both cheeks. The daughter of Amman's elder sister, Shireen Khala, Fazila had grown up in 'Pindi. When we were younger, she and her older brothers, Omar and Javed, used to visit Karachi, or we spent time with each other when my family flew up north. Fazila tinkered with dolls and fussed over clothing, while I played cricket with the boys. She now owned a clothing boutique on Zamzama, a new shopping district in Defense, and had helped me select clothes that she exclaimed would "suit your tiny figure perfectly." She herself was large-boned, her weight making her body sensual. To my suggestions that we walk in the evenings at Gymkhana, she flapped her hand and said: "Too hot."

Now leaning against the bed, Fazila regarded her ringed fingers with the feline quality she used to have when she was little and which no amount of childbearing or aging would change. "The city's quiet today. No bomb blasts, so I suppose we can go..." Fazila's tone was light, but she was referring to the violence that had escalated during the 1990's when Karachi had been torn apart by civil war.

The Sindhi-Muhajir tension had subsided, but everyone knew that more violence festered. For the short-term, life was unpredictable. Robberies occurred on a regular basis. Around the city, banks and stores hired armed guards with machine guns to sit at entry points to prevent break-ins. All our friends had stories to tell about robberies in homes or cars. "Just cooperate with thieves," was the advice that was offered to me multiple times. "Don't resist someone who's desperate with an automatic in his hand."

And yet, in the midst of the violence, people lived, ate, shopped, drank (all kinds of liquids ranging from bootlegged whiskey to home-grown wine), and attended weddings and dinners. Life felt familiar to me, having lived through curfews and martial law when I was a teenager, while the children were caught up with cousins and outings, remaining unaware of the discontent around us.

"Shall we go or shall we relax with our nimboo-paani?" She sipped the lemon-water that the maid Aneela had brought in.
Saira entered my room, clad in a new shalwar kurta, ready to explore the local markets.

"Let's go to the market," I responded, standing up.

*   *   *

Saira held my hand as we walked through a narrow street in Bohri Bazaar, a narrow-lane market where no cars could enter. I wrapped my arms around her, but left my elbows jutting out, instinctive self-defense that I had learned while visiting the bazaar as a teenager.

Some of my older female cousins used to hold open safety pins, ready to stab men who pushed against their bodies. I tensed as a man passed me, but he moved away without glancing at our group.

I relaxed as I registered the open space around us. Store-owners invited us to enter their stalls, but no one whistled or catcalled. From the market, we could hear puttering rickshaws, motorcycles, and buses that clogged the main roads, but Bohri Bazaar was quiet in the afternoon especially since air-conditioned shopping centers had opened in all parts of town, eliminating the need for trips to the trafficked, smog-infested, and violence-prone city center. The sun was strong, but naked lamps dangled inside stores, creating a contrast between shimmering bangles and cloth tarps.

Fazila watched Saira and me and smiled. "You foreign-returns! We didn't need to come here. You can buy bangles and slippers in Clifton."

Fazila's comment about the "foreign-returns" stung. None of my relatives or Amman's friends wore hundred-rupee glass bangles anymore; instead, all women my age were adorned with gold, rubies, emeralds, and diamonds. Ignoring Fazila's amusement, I urged Saira to select bangles she liked.

"Baji, we have best," urged the young boy manning the stand.

"Look out!" shouted Saira.

We pressed our bodies against a glass case as a man with a scale straddled over his shoulders, swung his pole, almost toppling the dates that he was trying to sell.

I returned my attention to the bangles. Six light bulbs burned over the boy's head highlighting the blue, red, and purple glass bangles that were decorated with gold and silver glitter and lined the walls of his three-foot stall. I held out my hand and asked the boy to give me two dozen from a leaf-green set that matched my outfit.

The boy felt my closed fist to assess my size and nodded. "Baji, you wear small size," he said. Counting two dozen bangles, he held my hand, pressed my thumb and my fingertips together, and teased the glass bangles onto my wrist, six at a time.

Fazila leaned against the case. "You're lucky," she said. "They look good on you. I have to wear big ones—the small sizes always break on me no matter how good those guys are…"

I was glad that despite all the Islamization around us, one aspect of bangle-buying had not changed: store-keepers, wizards at coaxing bangles onto the largest hands, could squeeze bangles on a woman's hand in public and not raise eyebrows. In appreciation of the boy's skill, I shook out my arm, making glass dance on my forearm.

Saira laughed at the tinkling sound.

"Pick some," I urged her.

She chose pomegranate pink, lined with silver, and the boy slid the glass past her tensed hand. Entranced by the glass loops on her forearm, Saira forgot about the noise and dust until her eyes fell on a bearded man who sat beneath a neem tree and rattled his bowl, asking for money. Saira shrank into a store lined with plastic buckets and straw brooms. Ignoring Fazila's 'foreign-return' look, I dropped ten rupees in the man's dish.

"If you want to help addicts, you should stop by the Edhi Foundation," Fazila said. "Poppy trade is out of control—I know many families who've been impacted by opium and heroin users."

I glanced toward Saira, and Fazila fell quiet.

* * *

Back at Fazila's house, Saira wandered off to join Nadia, Fazila's fourteen-year-old daughter, while Fazila and I flopped on a carved swing-bed. I ran my fingers along the bed's wooden rail, embossed with ivory. "What a beautiful bed!"

Fazila smiled. "Belonged to my mother-in-law. She died while sleeping in it, you know. I don't mind. She was so challenging when she was alive—inheriting this swing makes up for the difficult time she gave me. Though she did soften as she aged."

We leaned against velvet cushion covers, our legs dangling over the six-inch rail as we swung the bed back and forth. I remembered Fazila's mother-in-law, an oversized woman who criticized the weather, food, or anything that didn't measure up to her standard.

"So tell me, how are things there? We're hearing scary stories: desis being fired, thrown into jail, harassed at airports, getting beaten up. And getting deported, no? Is that why you came back now?"

Fazila's question was one that everyone asked. But in Houston before leaving for Karachi, I had been inundated with comments such as "You're going there?" as if Karachi were situated next to Kabul, which was being bombarded by US bombs and drone attacks. In Karachi, the conversation centered around the challenges Muslims faced in the US after the collapse of the Twin Towers. Post 9/11 changes had impacted Fazila's family: Admitted to a private college in New York, her eldest son had been waiting several months to gain a visa interview date at the US Embassy in Islamabad. She wasn't sure if he would be able to start college in the fall.

"Saira had some problems at school," I said. "I also wanted to see all of you. And I wanted the kids to experience life here."

"So why'd you stay away so long?" she asked. "You can move back and forth without hassle."

I sat up, making the bed lurch. Fazila was the first person to ask me the question—and expect a response. Other family members had deplored my absence and expressed appreciation that I had returned.

"Is it because you and your mother fought after Yasir...?"

I sipped lemon water that suddenly tasted too sharp.

Fazila shook her head. "Now you're silent. Just like you used to be when you were little. Always going off and talking to your animals, instead of to people."

"I'm not angry." My voice was low. "I was young. I dealt by leaving. I didn't know what I was doing."

"That must have been so tough to be alone. I'm glad you came back." Fazila squeezed my hand. "We don't have to talk about that time."

I nodded.

"How did you feel being married to a gora American?"

Her comment clung to my skin as if it were an oil slick from Kemari harbor. "Jim was Catholic!" I retorted. "He was circumcised. So in that sense, his penis was just like a Pakistani man's—except the color, of course."

Fazila threw her head back and laughed. "You would put it so bluntly."

Her hilarity melted my irritation. Everyone's curiosity was to be expected. As far as family was concerned, my life was their business. After all, the circumstances around Fazila's marriage were open knowledge, and she saw no reason why events in my life should be hidden.

Fazila was still waiting. "Seriously, how was it?"

I shrugged. "He was more closed. Or maybe that was just his personality. Being with Jim made me forget who I was."

"So that's why you stayed away."

I glanced out of the screen window at the jasmine vine outside. By nightfall, the flowers would blossom and the room would be filled with jasmine fragrance. Being an outsider was a familiar feeling—I had felt the same while growing up in Karachi, except that Yasir and I had created our own world. I made few friends at the coed upscale school that we attended, while Yasir found friends with whom he smoked cigarettes and hash during the year before he passed.

"I always liked you," Fazila said. "Even though you were secretive—different from Yasir. He was social and he knew how to listen. But you liked being alone or with your pets—used to drive me crazy when visited from 'Pindi. Everyone used to say, 'You'll have Yasmeen to play with.' But when I got here, you weren't around."

I had never seen my behavior from Fazila's perspective. To me, she had been the feminine cousin from the north. While growing up, I stayed away from extended family, but on this trip, I was reaching out to cousins—and the kids loved hanging out with Fazila's children.

She patted my arm. "I often thought about you. And your children are so wonderful—so well-mannered. I thought they'd be brats."

We laughed together.

"I used to envy you. I know things were rough for you. Losing Yasir... But you're lucky you went abroad to college. I don't know what I was thinking of when I accepted Muzaffar's proposal. I was only eighteen. And no one forced me. You know the story."

I nodded. Fazila's wedding, six months after Yasir's accident, was the last gathering I attended before leaving for college. One of her friend's brothers had seen her at a wedding and the next day, his mother delivered a marriage proposal to Fazila's parents. I remembered Fazila's mother, Shireen Khala, discussing the proposal with Amman. Fazila was right. No one had forced her to accept, but she was charmed by Muzaffar, and she didn't think twice about leaving her family and moving to Karachi where Muzaffar lived with his family. Her parents even tried to dissuade her, telling her that she could get engaged but wait a few years before formalizing the marriage. Fazila, entranced by the idea of a wedding which would be the talk of 'Pindi for years to come, didn't listen. She told her parents that she would join Karachi University after moving. Instead, by age nineteen, she became a full-time wife and mother.

Fazila regarded her painted toenails. "I don't regret my marriage. Muzaffar's a wonderful husband, but sometimes I'd think of you on the other side of the world, learning and meeting people. That made me wish that I hadn't been in such a hurry. Marriage is always available when you want it. I'd have loved to have studied philosophy. Or law."

"Law?"

"I've read some of Muzaffar's textbooks. Interesting."

Fazila was sharing a side of herself that I'd never known. The cousin whom I had dismissed as frilly had ambition. "Maybe you can. Education—like marriage—is also always there. When I go back to Houston, you can visit. Take a course or something."

A smile lingered around Fazila's mouth. "That's nice of you." She paused. "I thought you were going to look for jobs here?

"Jobs—in Karachi?" Another one of Amman's rumors.

"Yes. That's what your mother said. Something in teaching?"

"I just threw out an idea to Amman one day. And you know our mothers. She took my statement and ran with it. I'm going to have to return to Houston. Jim will send an international team to bring me back if we don't return before the kids' school starts. I had to make a deal with him and his lawyer just to come here for the summer." I rolled my eyes. "But I meant what I said about Houston."

"Let's see. I have the boutique. And the kids. Let's not worry about that. I wanted to know when you were going to 'Pindi. I may go with you. It's off-season at the shop, and Muzaffar's busy with some cases. Maybe we could go to Hawagali—like in the old days. Everyone says that the hill stations are safe..."

I smiled, surprised at the unexpected pleasure that the thought of traveling with her gave me.

twenty

YASMEEN

I leaned in the garden chair in Shireen Khala's Islamabad lawn, blew a smoke-ring, and watched it disintegrate in a gust of air. Squatting at the bottom of the Margalla Hills, the twin cities Islamabad and 'Pindi were basking in mild weather; our arrival in Islamabad had been heralded by a torrential downpour.

"A good omen," Amman had said when our plane hit the runway.

I nodded, remembering enough about Islamabad to know that without the rain, Islamabad's summertime heat—day or night—would have been suffocating.

Even though Shireen Khala's garden was walled, I could see the undulating ridge of the Margalla Hills, smooth like a green dinosaur's back. The frontier hills gave no hint of three colliding ranges, the Himalayas, Karakoram, and Hindukush, in the distance with peaks that pushed so high that the tops of the ranges couldn't be seen. A cloud darkened part of the mountain ridge, reminding me of Hawagali's shifting light.

Shireen Khala emerged through the front door, wearing a turquoise sari. Jasmine flowers threaded her earrings while keys jangled from her waist. Not one hair was out of place. I had never seen her dressed in anything other than a sari, with bangles on her wrists and keys at her waist. No matter where we were—in her 'Pindi house, in Karachi, or even Hawagali—Shireen Khala never appeared until she was fully dressed. When we were little, Yasir and I joked that she slept in a sari. As we got older, we used to wonder if she had sex wearing a sari.

A few years older than Amman, Shireen Khala and Amman were close. During my teenage years, much as I loved having a twin, when I saw Shireen Khala and Amman together, I used to wish that I had a sister with whom I could have a similar relationship. They even looked alike. Amman was taller, but both had long faces and wavy hair that they tried to contain. Shireen Khala succeeded in the effort, while Amman battled tendrils.

The woman walking behind Shireen Khala, a live-in maid called Hasina, set a tray on the table and squatted on the grass to pour us some hot tea. After serving us, she stood by the verandah doorway, her eyes fixed on Shireen Khala, ready to respond to any cue.

Oblivious of her audience, Shireen Khala said, "You're lucky the weather changed. It's never so cool in June."

I stirred the sugar and shot a glance toward Hasina. After so many years of living in the US, where I paid a weekly cleaning woman to scrub the house while I was at work, I was reminded of how in Pakistan, privacy was a foreign concept. I could write a book about the differences and paradoxes between the two spaces. In the US, I never understood the structure of homes where living room windows faced the streets whereas in South Asia, the homes of rich people were barred from public eye by eight feet high walls, but all action occurring in residential homes was public knowledge. Neither lifestyle made sense, and I couldn't pick which structure I liked better. I used to wish that I could find a way to mix and match splices from each region to create a new country.

None of my thoughts affected Shireen Khala as she sipped her tea. "You know that Sikandar Bhai just left Islamabad. He was getting the Hawagali house ready—they're working on the plumbing. He thinks that we can drive there in a week. In the meantime, I thought that we could visit Taxila for a day. You haven't seen the ruins for a while. It's quiet there now. In December we would have heard American warplanes all the time..."

I had been to Taxila with Shireen Khala and Uncle Moeen before. When we were younger, Yasir and I often wished that our parents were more like Amman's sister and her husband—they planned picnics, parties, and outings together. In contrast, events in our household were always one-sided with Amman planning and Abu rarely joining in.

Shireen Khala continued: "They've excavated all the sites, so some will be new to you. My favorite ones are the ruins of a Buddhist monastery—Jaulian. The monastery is on a hill with beautiful friezes. Worth looking at."

I nodded in agreement.

"Very well, I'll make preparations for us to visit Taxila tomorrow." She stood up, and Hasina jumped forward to draw her mistress' chair back. Once Shireen Khala was out of sight, Hasina began to gather up the tray.

I held out my arm to stop her. "I'll bring it in."

Hasina rose and disappeared into the house.

*   *   *

Taxila museum had not changed since my last visit. A rectangular building, the museum was filled with statues that had been excavated from ruins that were three thousand years old. While I gazed at the friezes, which marked the birth of Buddhism, the children—just like Yasir and I had done thirty years ago—raced each other in the lawn.

Once finished with the museum, Shireen Khala and I joined Moeen Uncle, Fazila, and Amman who relaxed in the shade.

After a while, Shireen Khala stood up. "If we're going to the monastery, we should visit before it gets too hot." Her keys jangled as she stood up. "Who wants to join me?"

Peeping one eye from beneath the dupatta that she was using to protect herself from the sun, Amman shook her head. Fazila and Uncle Moeen didn't bother to look up. I forced myself to rise. The afternoon sun was hot, but I knew that the ruins would be worth the visit.

Since the driver was eating a late lunch at the adjoining village, Shireen Khala moved behind the steering wheel and drove down the dirt road. I bit my cuticles, wondering if I should have remained in the garden with everyone else. Shireen Khala's sternness intimidated me. I wondered what she thought about my estrangement from Amman. She would not have put up with distancing from her children.

Parking the car in front of a canteen beneath the Jaulian hill, she walked toward the torn tarp beneath which chairs and tables were strewn. Three men sat on benches and watched us. Seeing Shireen Khala, they leapt up to salute her. The man with the curliest mustache pulled out a 7-Up bottle from a tin canister and clinked it with the bottle opener.

"On the way back!" smiled Shireen Khala.

"Are you needing guide today, Madam?" the man asked.

She shook her head and exchanged a few more pleasantries with the man, Khan, after which she and I began our ascent up the winding pathway.

"Khan's son works in Moeen's office," Shireen Khala explained. "He's a good man. He's been here a long time—cares for the ruins more than he loves his family."

"They know you well. Do you visit the ruins by yourself?"

Shireen Khala stepped up the stairs one at a time, lifting her sari edge to protect the rim from dirt, revealing her toe-rings. "As often as I can."

I followed her up the stairs. Stepping over fallen stones and branches, Shireen Khala reached the top without breaking sweat, but I was out of breath.

"Yoga," she explained.

"Aren't you hot?" I asked.

"All in the mind, dear," she said, ignoring my tone. "Imagine yourself in a deep freezer and you'll feel that way. Instant air-conditioning from the inside."

I held back from responding, wishing for one time when I could see Shireen Khala out of control. Even on the day after Yasir's accident, she appeared and swept through the house, taking charge, and restoring order to our lives. She arranged for his body to be driven to 'Pindi and buried in the family graveyard, and three days later, arranged the soyem in 'Pindi.

A tall man at the gate entrance salaamed her, seeming to know her well. She introduced me and his creased face lit up. "From America, Madam? Enjoy your visit."

We entered a covered courtyard with sandstone floors and ceilings. Around us were the many faces of Buddha, which had endured more than three thousand years of storms, rain, and earthquakes. In the center of the covered area was a mound, decorated with Buddhist motifs and friezes. We walked around the block in the center and up a set of low stairs to find ourselves in an uncovered courtyard that used to be a dining hall or prayer room, but the walls had eroded over the years. Walking to the edge, I gazed at the valley and blue mountains. I sucked in my breath, appreciating the view that the monastery windows had once overlooked. No wonder that centuries ago the Greeks had chosen to make northern Pakistan their home.

We returned to the covered area, where good training—and Shireen Khala's presence—prevented me from tracing my hands over the sculptures. We were alone in the ruins until my eyes caught sight of a woman in a dark shalwar kurta, who darted up the stairs into the open courtyard above. Despite goose-bumps on my arm, I decided to follow the figure upstairs. But when I reached the open courtyard, I saw only the sand-swept floor and unbroken sky.

I turned to Shireen Khala, who was behind me. "Did you see her?"

"The woman?"

"Yes. Where'd she go?"

Shireen Khala looked around. "I'm not sure."

The courtyard was empty. I frowned. The only way for the woman to leave the courtyard was by descending through the passageway where I stood, but no one had passed me. I returned to the covered area—the woman had to be somewhere. As I circled the large statue, I couldn't shake the feeling of being watched, but no one was around.

"Did someone else come inside?" I asked the chowkidar.

The guard glanced at Shireen Khala. "No, Madam."

"Are you sure?" I insisted. "Could someone have come up the hillside?"

He smiled. "No one climbs that way, Madam. The gully is deep."

As we descended the stairs and turned a corner, a man blocked us. I expelled a low scream.

Shireen Khala placed a hand on my arm. "He's selling statues. This is Khalid. He and his family have been replicating statues for generations."

Khalid greeted Shireen Khala and fell into step behind us. Reaching into his pocket, he drew out sandstone and black granite replicas of the Buddha. By the time we reached the bottom of the hill, I was the owner of four sculptures: one for me, one for Janet, and one for Carlos. I also bought a seated sandstone Buddha for Amman.

Dizzy from the heat, I sat beneath the tarp and sipped a cold drink. "That woman. I could've sworn she was there. And when Khalid jumped out from behind the tree—I thought he was a... a ghost."

Shireen Khala smiled with her lips closed. "These are ruins you know. Generations have moved through this space. If only they could tell us what they have witnessed. Taxila is a magical place."

I looked around us, conscious of the group of men who sat on a roped wooden bed across from us and watched us as they talked amidst each other. I had to remind myself that people-watching was a national pastime, especially when outsiders surfaced. "Do you feel safe? Ever since the first war erupted in Afghanistan people have been armed to the teeth..."

Shireen Khala shook her head. "These days, the landscape is different, especially with the warplanes flying toward Afghanistan. But we live here. Whenever visitors arrive, I bring them to Taxila—unless there's serious political upheaval. I also visit the site alone—it's so peaceful and I never know what I'm going to find."

"Like that woman?"

"Like that woman," she repeated. "I've never seen her before."

"You're always so calm about everything!" The words left my mouth before I could contain myself.

To my surprise, Shireen Khala didn't scold me. Instead, she patted my arm. "You can be upset, Baita. I can see why you would want answers. When you were little, I used to tell your mother that your biggest strength was your passion—your desire to dig out the truth."

I felt my anger dissipate like steam from a kettle. Even though Shireen Khala's temperament was different from mine, she had supported me. I remembered one time when Abu accused the driver of stealing mangos from our tree to sell them, and Yasir and I defended him. Shireen Khala, who was visiting us, stood by our side and helped us overrule Abu's accusations. "You're always so calm—makes me think that you don't want answers. That you look down on me for wanting to know more." I sniffled my tears.

Shireen Khala placed her palm on my elbow. "It's not that I don't want to know—or that I think less of you because you want to. I find comfort by accepting that I cannot find answers to everything." She frowned. "This woman, though, she was modern."

I shivered again. "Her movement reminded me of Kaneez Bua and those kaneez stories."

Shireen Khala clicked her tongue. "Poor Kaneez. I never understood why my cousin Babur transformed her into a witch. She always looked after us. She never learned how to smile, so we converted her into a witch. We never appreciated her. The mountain myth draws upon the whole idea of women masking themselves and being double-faced. But I have to remind myself that Babur fabricated the story, and we believed him. Nothing more, and nothing less. And your mother and I, we passed the narrative to your generation—just as you're probably repeating with your children."

"But you believed the stories when you were little."

"Just as you did. But we can set Kaneez aside since we're older and know better."

I placed my 7-Up bottle on the wooden bench and twisted the paper straw between my fingers. I knew that the moment in Taxila could be converted into a story that I would share with my children, and that I would probably change the narrative to be more mysterious.

Shireen Khala tapped my hand and brought me back to the moment. "Baita, you and your mother must put your brother to rest. All these years, I've watched your mother blame herself. Why? We have grieved enough."

I pulled open the car door. "He wouldn't have gone out if he hadn't been looking for her."

"Yes. And you've been reminding her all these years. Let it go. I was happy when she went to see you and to learn that you had patched things up. Are you still holding on?"

On the drive to the museum, I swathed my dupatta around my face to prevent dust from filtering into my nostrils, keeping my eyes fixed on mustard fields lined with wild marijuana.

Shireen Khala drove fast, her hands gripping the top of the wheel. I closed my eyes and thought about how Shireen Khala's house—unlike those of other family members where Yasir's photograph could be seen in living rooms—displayed only one photo of Yasir, and it was tucked in her study.

twenty-one

YASMEEN

"Are we going to see kaneezes?" Sam asked. He was the first child to appear at the breakfast table and was shoveling his egg and paratha before we piled into cars to drive toward Hawagali.

"And cobra plants?" Saira threw in. Her face wasn't hidden by her hair. Amman had braided Saira's hair, something she'd been wanting to do since she first met her granddaughter in Houston.

"How long will we stay there?" Fazila asked.

"Two weeks," Amman said. She had visited Yasir's grave earlier in the morning.

Fazila looked up from the paper. "Two weeks! What are we going to do there for so long? There's no TV."

She succeeded in getting her mother to purse her lips. "We'll go for walks. Enjoy nature."

"Might be boring. We'll take breaks and go people-watching in Murree, right, Yasmeen?" Fazila winked at me and dug her elbow in my side. I nodded, suppressing my laughter. Amman's glance met Fazila's laughing eyes and her irritation melted.

* * *

"Our politicians are perpetually stoned," drawled Uncle Moeen from behind the wheel. "Do you wonder why?" He waved his hand at the marijuana that grew wild, lining the mountain road that led to the mountains. We were behind an oil truck that had a psychedelic mountain landscape painted on the rear of its circular tank. I loved how each piece of transport had transformed into public art. Beneath the painted image of mountains and water streams was a verse inscribed in calligraphic Urdu.

Uncle Moeen turned off toward the mountains. The truck driver flapped his hand out of his window, giving us permission to pass him. The road was wider than when we used to visit the north.

Reading my mind, Fazila laughed. "Rumor has it one of our senior politicians was having an affair with a woman who has a house in Murree. He had the roads widened and repaved. So now we get to drive in comfort."

Our first stop, like always, was Murree, a hill station that the British had cultivated as a respite from city heat. Urban crowds thronged narrow cobbled streets, a different sight from the quiet mountain village that I remembered. We stopped to dine at Mountain View, an old favorite restaurant. Women strolled in, wearing high heels. Their painted fingernails, jewelry, and silken dupattas could be found anywhere in the world—Karachi, Hong Kong, or New York— but the chaos around us didn't fit into my memory of Murree, nor did I feel as if we were six thousand feet up in the mountains.

The views had also changed. Where once dense fir forests had been visible from the restaurant windows, our eyes now fell on denuded mountain sides and concrete houses. But one aspect remained the same. From the window, I could see—between strolling tourists— men hauling burlap sacks filled with rice and flour, women sweeping streets, and children in rags, begging for food or change.

Catching my expression, Uncle Moeen nudged me. "Don't say I didn't warn you." He was looking at the city travelers.

Fazila also paid little attention to the underbelly of poverty—the sight was too familiar. "I come here for people watching," she said.

Amman and Shireen Khala chose seats facing the wall and ordered their meal.

"Why can't they just go back to the cities?" muttered Shireen Khala.

After Murree, the road was narrow and bumpy, and I had to grip the dashboard. I had switched cars to ride with Amman, Fazila and Shireen Khala, while Uncle Moeen packed his car with the children. Our driver's shoulders were hunched. Every few minutes, he beeped his horn to inform a motorcyclist or a bus driver to move aside so we could pass. Once, as he took a swerving turn, he nearly hit a descending bus, but he managed to squeeze uphill without any casualties. A swirling mist, caused by clouds, was building around the narrow road with sections that were broken by water streams caused by recent rain.

A young boy stood to the side along with his three goats, waiting for our car to pass. Looking above, I caught sight of a monkey perched on a fir tree branch at the base of which were cobra plants. I rolled down my window, inhaling the air. "Nothing's changed," I whispered, more to myself than to Fazila, Amman, and Shireen Khala who were in the back.

We passed through Ghoragali, Dungagali, and Nathiagali. The road wound higher toward Hawagali, the highest hill station that overlooked the Himalayas. The driver turned a corner to pass through the Hawagali market area. The sun burst out from behind the clouds, drenching the street with light, spilling onto melons and vegetable stands. Smoke rose from oil heating in open pans. Men wearing northern style hats stepped away from the street to avoid getting splashed. Hawagali was more crowded, but the village looked the same. The car ascended, leaving behind the market, moving toward hotels and houses. We turned on the road between the double-storied hourse and the park.

"Looks tiny!" Fazila said. She was right. The house looked dark and small, while the park looked like a platter rather than a bowl with steep slopes that I remembered. Daffodils, daisies, buttercups, and dandelions lined the park's slopes, but plastic bags, coke bottles, and Frooto cartons were strewn along the stairs that led to the bottom of the park.

Hawagali's scent, fir mingled with burning wood, saturated my nostrils. The car spiraled upward. I started. From behind an oak tree, I saw a long thin face. A young man with curly hair. Sunlight, like the sweep of a flashlight, dwelled on the face, alive with laughter. Grabbing the car handle, I twisted my head, but the boy had vanished.

The hide-and-seek quality of Hawagali still had a grip on me. In the back seat, Amman's head lolled against Fazila's shoulder, not yet awake to our moment of arrival, but Shireen Khala smiled.

The driver turned the car up the steep road leading to the house.

Everything looked the same except more stone cottages lined the hillside. Some, like our house, were old, painted green with sections of corrugated steel roofs and chimneys. Amman sat up.

I remembered a summer from many years ago when Yasir and I were the same age as my children, and we drove to Hawagali after an identical lunch and dessert in Murree with Abu behind the wheel. Yasir and I pushed our faces out of the windows, trying to ignore Amman and Abu who sat in the front, silently fighting with each other. As soon as the car turned up the steep road, cool clouds blew through the car windows and swept the anger away. Abu reached over and tucked an escaped strand of Amman's hair behind her ear. She smiled at him—no one could stay detached or angry on this last stretch before we reached our house.

Almost three decades later, Amman sat upright in the car, her tiredness faded as breeze blew though the car. She leaned forward, her hands gripping the back of the driver's seat. Fazila's face was serene, while Shireen Khala rested her head back. The driver took one last turn, making my heart bounce like a ping-pong ball against my chest.

We were at the gates of the house near the quarters where Heera and her grandfather once lived. The new chowkidar salaamed us and pushed open the gates. Our cars rolled up the driveway toward our house. Behind the house, clouds swirled as if we were in a painting. The stump where Athar had once waited for us to bring Mithoo had been polished to make a seat. New fir saplings sprouted by the front door.

I stepped out of the car. The children raced toward me and flung themselves in my arms.

"Mom, we saw your park!" Sam asked. "And I saw a kaneez!"

"I saw cobra plants," volunteered Saira. "They weren't scary."

Holding hands, we stepped inside the house. Wood floors resounded beneath our footsteps, shaking history loose, reminding me of the years when I lived for this moment, arriving hot and tired from Karachi to have my energy restored by mountain breeze. The children chugged through the rooms, pushing on each other's shoulders like a train.

I wandered into the attic tucked beneath the sloping roof. The attic had more light and the view from the window was no longer obstructed by the oak in which we were convinced that the kaneezes

170

lived. Peering out of the window, I saw a splintered trunk below, the result of a lightning storm. I shivered. This was the room where Shireen Khala and Amman first encountered the kaneezes with their cousin Babur, and where Yasir used to box the punching bag that Abu bought for him.

Fazila's shoulders touched mine. She glanced around the room. "They knocked out the bedroom."

I nodded. I had never slept in the attic bedroom, but Yasir used to crash upstairs. Fazila was right: The room partition had been removed, and the attic stretched over the length of the house, except for the section that was above the kitchen. One window revealed the kitchen's corrugated roof and chimney.

Fazila interrupted my thoughts. "I used to wait for the sound of raindrops to hit the roof."

I smiled. Yasir and I used to do the same, the rainwater making us feel as if we were in a drumming concert that had been choreographed for us. I wondered how I would feel about the rain given my last summer at the house.

Seeing me light a cigarette, Fazila held out her hand.

I offered her the case. "I didn't know you smoked."

"I don't. This is where I smoked my first—with your twin."

"You and Yasir spent time here? Together?" I could hear the hurt in my voice.

"That surprises you?" Fazila took a puff and blew the smoke out as if she were spitting dust balls. "Just once, a long time ago. The proposal had come in from Muzaffar's family and everyone— especially your mother—was telling me not to rush. I came up here crying to get away from the noise. Yasir was on the floor cross-legged as if he was meditating. Of course, he was smoking. Cigarettes and hash. He asked me to join him." She closed her eyes.

Yasir had never mentioned the encounter. "You smoked with Yasir? Hash?" I had to stop repeating everything she said.

"I just wanted to try it." Fazila sounded defensive. "I was sick of everything. And he offered me some. 'This should help,' he said. I got along with Yasir, you know. He and I understood each other."

My eyes fell on a marble ashtray that lay upon a chest of drawers. I stubbed my cigarette.

"I told him why I was crying. He asked me to hold out my palm and traced his finger along my heart line and told me that I had a strong heart. 'Listen to your heart. Not your Amman or mine,' he said. 'You don't have to repeat their mistakes.' And that was the day, young as I was, when I decided to marry Muzaffar. Yasir helped me decide. He was an excellent listener, the best in our family."

I remembered the times when Yasir listened to me talking about what was bothering me: Mithoo, Amman, Abu, school, homework. I nodded. "He was good."

"He and I talked that afternoon—and after that day, other afternoons. Well, I talked and he listened. I told him, 'I feel guilty because everyone wants me to have a career, and I want children and a family. Stability.' 'Go for it,' he told me. And that's what I did. You know, I often wondered about him. He sounded as if he understood about love. But he didn't ever have a girlfriend, did he?"

I shook my head. "Just a crush on this girl at our school. Nothing serious. I used to like her brother. We were all part of the same group— and went to movies and parties together."

Fazila laughed. "What if you had both married in the same family?" Her face fell. "But you chose an American and he..."

"Did you ever talk about anything else?"

"Not really." Her eyes shifted away from mine.

"Tell me!"

"He said that if I were to marry Muzaffar, I had to be sure that I loved him. 'You don't want to become like Amman,' he said. And I knew what he was talking about. Laila Khala was unhappy. I always knew there was someone else, but everyone forced her to marry your father. I told Yasir there wasn't anyone else. That I liked Muzaffar. 'Then follow your heart,' he said."

I leaned into the window, conscious of my tears building up.

Fazila sighed. "You're not the only one who feels guilty about Yasir. I could have helped him. One time, I came upstairs, and he was messing with opium. The drama series, Traffik hadn't even been filmed at that time. I didn't know anything about opium in the northern areas, and how the market had exploded during the Zia years. Yasir saw my face, and he put it away."

I turned around. "You're telling me that he... was an opium addict?"

She shook her head. "No—he said he tried it a few times. 'It's not a big deal,' he told me. 'I don't even buy the stuff.' But I should have told your mother..."

The children's voices floated up from the garden. "Or you could have said something to me..."

Nadia raised her voice from below: "Don't leave the grounds without permission," she called out. "And don't talk to strangers."

"Acha," Sameer replied in Urdu.

At first I thought that my cheeks were wet because of the clouds that had rolled through, but when moisture hit my lips, I realized that the water was salty.

*   *   *

I push through the mist. Carlos holds my arm in the pitch black. We race through the piney forest, looking for Yasir, searching in the bushes, and behind the trees. Branches slap our faces, tearing gashes in our cheeks. From above, quavering screams splinter the forest. The kaneezes with their yellow lantern eyes fly above Carlos and me, their wings flap close, lift my hair, pluck my earrings, stir the air around us, and tangle my hair.

My hair is broken glass and ice, pricking my body, making me cry, causing my eyes to bleed, and scratching scars along my forehead and nose. I lose Carlos' hand. The witches pull at my ears, tearing off earrings, their eyes glow. Through blood streaming down my face, I look for my twin, but an ice fragment blinds my eye. Trees become still. A kaneez's wing shrouds my face, mops blood, and releases glass from my eye. I cry as if I will never stop, knowing, with the certainty that one can only have in one's dream, that I have lost Yasir to the kaneezes above.

*   *   *

Emerging from a nightmare, I sat up in bed and opened my eyes in a room that was darker than the insides of my eyelids. From beneath my pillow, I pulled out the flashlight—a lesson learned from Yasir's accident—that Uncle Moeen had given each of us. Fazila stirred and turned over to pull the cover over her face. Once her breath returned to normal, I padded across the hallway into the room that Sameer shared with Arif.

In Sameer's room—I had begun calling him by his full name since we'd arrived in Hawagali—I covered my flashlight with my shawl to

173

dim its bulb. The sleeping boys lay in twin beds; Arif was turned on his stomach, face buried in his pillow, while Sameer lay on his back, palm open, fingers curled. I watched him breathe. I returned to my room and lay down, still unable to sleep.

When I fell asleep, my rest was dreamless.

twenty-two

YASMEEN

I awakened early and set out for a solitary walk, allowing sunlight to melt the nightmares from my eyelashes.

Over breakfast, when I told Fazila about my dream, she fell silent. "I'd be careful if I were you," she said. "Don't bring bad karma into this trip."

Amman bustled around the kitchen ordering sandwiches and pastries, expecting Heera for tea. When Heera arrived, Amman opened her arms to welcome her friend with kisses on both cheeks. The women reentered the house, holding hands like teenage girls. Heera, tall and straight-backed, had a slight limp from polio. She wore her hair in a braid as she used to when I last saw her, except that her black hair had turned silver. Yasir and I used to tug her hair as if it were a horse's tail. She smiled at me, her lips looking as if rose petals had landed on her face.

"You've become thin," she said. Her voice had acquired a steely edge from years of working in the classroom and telling girls how to behave.

At the table we—five women joined by blood and history—sipped tea. When Saira and Sameer returned from their horse-riding lessons, they allowed Heera to hug them. She opened her purse to offer them treats.

With a lollipop in his mouth, Sameer clamored for a story. "Nani,

175

it's been ages," he said, his eyes looking blacker than usual. "How about another story?

Amman glanced at Heera. "Today, maybe Heera Aunty will tell you a story."

Heera's cheeks reddened. "I'm not very good at that..."

Amman prodded Heera's knee with her slipper. "Tell them about the time..."

"The time I got lost?" Heera completed Amman's sentence. Heera leaned in her chair, knitting her palms behind her head. "I'm not a storyteller like your Nani, but I'll try.

"When I was fifteen, I misplaced a book that your Nani loaned me. I remembered that I had left the book somewhere on the road between this house and Titlipark. I decided to go look for it. On my way, I saw a white dove that seemed to call me, so I chased it. But after a while, I lost sight of the bird's gleaming wings.

"But when I looked around me, I realized that I had lost my way. I was in the forest with trees so tall that I couldn't even see the sky. Something fell by my feet, and I heard a hooting sound. Looking up, I saw a monkey hurling pine cones at me. I covered my head and started to run. One of the pine cones hit my shoulder, another my head. So I picked one up and threw it back up into the trees. That's when I saw monkeys, more than I could count, sitting on tree branches and copying my screams as if they were parrots. I plugged my ears with my fingers and started to run, but their shouts got louder.

"As I ran, I noticed that the monkeys were gone. Instead, high in the trees, were shadows. I found myself in front of this house. I was shivering and shaking. After that time, I swore that I would never venture out alone again."

Saira sat back. "What were the shadows?"

Shrugging, Heera said, "I thought they were kaneezes. But now I know that no such thing exists. I think my fear created the noise and images because once I calmed down, the shadows melted. And the monkeys weren't vicious. They were having fun. In fact, after that day, they began to visit me and I fed them leftover naan."

Amman spoke up. "There are many stories about Hawagali. The truth is, you're fine as long as you stay on the roads, and never leave the house alone. You should never touch the cobra plants—they are poisonous—but other than that, there's nothing to be afraid of. Nothing at all."

I inhaled the pine scent around me, repeating to myself that everything was fine. But at night, my anxiety returned, buzzing around my ears like mosquitoes that refused to go away. Yasir had experienced the same moment that Heera had, but Yasir had not survived. I missed Carlos, the feel of his stubby hands on mine, his arms, his chest pressing against my body. If he were with me I would ask him to rock me to sleep.

*　*　*

"Take good care of your mother and your aunt," Uncle Moeen called. He reached out of the window and tickled Sameer's stomach. The car disappeared around the corner, whisking him to the city to his job, leaving us four women with the children. Amman and Shireen Khala moved between the kitchen and the living room, ordering groceries and planning meals, while I settled in the garden to sketch the landscape that I wanted to put on canvas. Immersed in shading and sketching the fish fountain and the flower garden, I didn't notice time passing until Sameer yanked the pencil out of my hand.

"Chalain?" he said, inviting me to the park, showing off a new Urdu word he had learned. Sameer's frame seemed to have stretched four inches since our arrival.

I hugged him and tucked away my sketch-book. On our way to the front of the house, I invited Fazila to join us, and was surprised when she agreed to abandon the final coat on her nails.

"Let this dry." She held her hands out for everyone to admire.

Her daughter Nadia, a tomboy in a t-shirt and jeans, rolled her eyes, but Saira with her hair in pigtails was captivated. She had already told me that when she grew up, she wanted to be like Fazila Khala. The thought no longer scared me as much as it once might have.

In the front hallway, Amman awaited us armed with a pile of woolies. "A sweater for everyone," she pronounced. "And umbrellas."

Used to her insistence, we complied, but Sameer pushed aside the blue sweater she thrust toward him. "Do I have to?" he grumbled. "It's hot."

I knew the sweater. Years ago, Amman had knitted it for Yasir; in Karachi, she had handed it to Sameer. At the time, Sameer had been honored to own something that once belonged to his uncle.

Amman shot him a look. "Take your sweater, young man. And look after it."

"But—"

"Take it! Let's go!" called Arif, stamping his foot.

Sameer pulled the blue bundle from Amman, and we headed outside. The children skipped ahead, racing to see who reached first. When we reached the park, they rolled down the slopes as if they were barrels. Amman and Shireen Khala took their knitting to the bottom of the hill and waited for Heera.

Fazila and I hovered at the rim of the park, neither of us wanting to sit. As we rounded the corner to pass by the double-storied house, I remembered the light I had glimpsed through its window during our first evening in Hawagali.

"Let's go and take a look," I suggested, the sunlight melting away anxieties from my dream world. "Maybe someone lives here."

Fazila nodded.

We walked up the pathway and knocked on the door of the house. To our surprise, the brass knob twisted open and we stepped into a dark room lit by sun rays streaming through a stained glass window. No one seemed to live in the space since there was no furniture, but the building was seeped with the scent of burning wood as if a stove or a fire had recently been lit somewhere in the building. I flicked my finger across a built-in shelf. It came away clean—no dust.

"Looks like someone's taking care of this place," Fazila said.

The flooring and the walls of the entrance lobby were dark. We allowed our eyes to explore the space, which we had never seen though we had spent many summers in Hawagali. On the ground in the corner lay a black cloth that looked like tar.

I stepped back.

Fazila shuffled her toes. "We should go. This place is creepy."

We heard shuffling and the creak of another door. Turning around, we saw an older woman standing in a doorway.

"Can I help you?" the woman asked. Her forehead was marked with grooves as deep as gorges. I couldn't tell where she was from.

I grabbed Fazila's arm, my fingernails digging into her flesh. The woman's hair was pulled into a straggly bun, gray with streaks of red henna. "Your return is overdue," she said in Urdu.

"I haven't been here since I was little," I said.

"Be careful." The woman took three steps toward us. "Someone close to your heart is in danger. Those who are haunted by fear are in danger."

Fazila took over. "Sorry to intrude. We have to leave now." She pulled at me.

I could see every groove around the woman's eyes and on her tree-bark forehead. The woman ignored Fazila. "Stay with me. I'll tell you how to be safe. How to make your loved ones safe."

"Let's go!" Fazila hissed, but the woman continued talking as if Fazila were not in the room.

"You have traveled a distance, leaving someone you love. Three men: a brother, a lover, and a son. Do not cross the line. You must choose."

Fazila dragged my arm, and I allowed her to pull me into the sunlight.

"My friend from America, I have missed you!" the woman crooned into the doorway.

Almost falling over each other, Fazila and I hurried to the house. The maid brought us water when we arrived. My hands shook, and Fazila wiped her forehead with her dupatta.

I found my voice. "This is completely crazy. How did she know so much about me?"

Fazila paced the room. "That was scary. I wonder why she talked only to you..."

"How did she know about Yasir? And about me visiting from the States?"

"You look different." She paused and glanced toward Hasina, the maid that had traveled with us from Islamabad. Hasina left the room without collecting our glasses. "I don't think we should allow the encounter to upset us. Remember what Heera said earlier—about fear being created in our minds?"

"You were scared too."

Fazila nodded. "Yes. Very scared. But we can't let this get to us. The woman was just guessing. She didn't know anything about us or you. I'm not going to stress out. I need a nap to recover..."

Her hair bounced as she headed up the stairs. When we were little, Yasir and I were the ones fascinated by Hawagali's folklore, but Fazila and her brothers dismissed the stories. My thoughts returned to the woman. She said someone I loved was in danger—Carlos, Sameer, Saira? Amman?

I shook my hair loose. Fazila was right. I couldn't let the encounter get to me, but I wanted to ask the woman to explain herself. I didn't need more unsolved mysteries in my life. Amman and the children were still at the park. I decided to return in that direction and see if I could talk to the woman again. If she turned out to be a fake psychic, I could dispel my anxieties. I grabbed a shawl from the chair and headed out before I changed my mind.

Seated on a bench in the bowl park, Amman, Shireen Khala, and Heera were engaged in conversation. The children, engrossed in a new version of cricket that they had invented that morning, expelled whoops of laughter.

I walked up the path to knock on the door of the house, but the heavy chestnut wood swallowed my knock as if I were tickling a mountain's shoulder. I knocked louder and turned the doorknob. The knob did not shift. Crows cawed from fir tree boughs that towered over the building. I walked along the pathway by the side of the house, thinking that perhaps the woman didn't hear my knock on the front door. But the side door was also locked, and my knock met with no response.

Feeling as if I were in one of Amman's stories, I returned to the park just as the children, Amman, and Heera ascended the staircase to return home. I fell in beside Sameer who straggled behind everyone, kicking stones. "What's wrong?" I asked.

He kicked a stone over the side of the road and watched it roll down the hillside and stop against an oak tree's root. "No TV. I miss Dad."

I hugged him. "Maybe you can call him later. I know he must be thinking of you, too."

Sameer pulled away from me. "Why can't you stay in the park with me? Dad would. Why can't we email him? And why does everyone call me 'Sameer'? I like 'Sam' better."

I patted his hand. "You know there's no email here." I kept my voice low. Sooner or later, he was bound to start missing Jim and his Houston life. "It's teatime now. Your Nani's baked a chocolate cake, and we have to be present. I promise I'll bring you back in the morning, okay? And we can call you Sam if you like, or we can switch back and forth. Both names belong to you."

He kicked another pebble. "Why can't I stay outside? I want to go to Houston."

I pulled him close. "I'm sorry, Sam. We'll return home soon."

Heera matched her pace with ours. "Is everything all right?"

I nodded.

"I saw you and Fazila earlier." She placed a hand on my shoulder.

My heartbeat slowed and the heat slipped from my face. Her students must love her. "I'll tell you when we get back." I glanced toward Sameer. Heera nodded.

*   *   *

The children played scrabble in the dining room. Running water gushed from the kitchen as Hasina washed the dishes.

Rested from her nap, Fazila entered the family room and poured herself a cup of tea. "Have you told them yet?" she asked.

I focused on the newspaper. "Why don't you tell them? Or maybe you don't think it was a big deal."

"Don't be sarcastic. It doesn't suit you." She turned to Amman, Heera, and Shireen Khala. "Yasmeen and I visited the abandoned house today. We saw a woman who gave us dire predictions. She called Yasmeen: 'my friend from America'..."

"She talked to me as if she knew me," I said.

Fazila looked around the room. "I admit. I was frightened. But we came home. I took a nap and woke up feeling better."

"But I went back."

Fazila's smile faded. "I didn't know that. Did you see the woman again?"

I shook my head.

Shireen Khala knit her brows together.

Heera said, "I heard something about a woman living at that house. She's supposed to be the caretaker. You didn't imagine her. She's said to be eccentric. I wouldn't worry about her."

"She knew I lived in the States," I said.

Heera's response was much like Fazila's. "She could have heard talk in the village. Don't forget your maid is from around here. You can't keep secrets in Hawagali." I noticed her shooting a glance toward Amman.

"We thought the woman was a kaneez," Fazila said.

"A kaneez!" Heera's voice was a bullet ricocheting in the air. "I wish someone would—how do you say?—deconstruct that legend.

What does the word refer to after all? Dupattas? Heads being covered? Women going against social norm? People always have to view women who act against custom as evil or as witches."

Thrilled at the academic turn of the discussion, Shireen Khala joined in. "So little is known about the Gallies and local mythology. I used to think that we'd made up that myth because of our Kaneez Bua. But I've talked to villagers, and there are legends about witches. They don't call them 'kaneezes' as we began to do in our family, but people here believe that witches roam the mountainside. If we examine the legend, we can view our Kaneez Bua—and their witches— as powerful women that people fear. They have wings and are capable of camouflage. Don't forget the Buraq, the winged creature that flew Prophet Mohammad to heaven... The Buraq's face is always portrayed as female."

Heera nodded. "Women with wings are fascinating and appear in multiple cultures. I've seen beautiful drawings of the Buraq."

Amman stared out of the window at the swaying oak tree. She was not thinking of women with wings. She had to have been thinking about how she used to cover herself with a chaddar to visit her lover. For her, the chaddar was not a tool of oppression—the fabric had given her anonymity.

"Does anyone remember what the word 'kaneez' means?" Fazila asked. "Slave-girl. Maybe people like to view powerful women as slaves, so they don't fear them."

"Excellent point," her mother approved. "And our Kaneez Bua— she never smiled, but she held our 'Pindi house together, especially when our father was going bankrupt. We relied on her. I don't understand why her name became synonymous with witch. Witches are frightening to those who don't wish to see women as independent."

Heera nodded. "I've lived here my entire life. I'm tired of people thinking that scant clothing means more freedom. Women should be allowed to wear what we want. And kaneezes—or the myth of them— are my friends. I go out at night alone, and I often feel as if the female energy in the mountains protects me."

Fazila shook her head. "I hate the idea of even having legends about women who cover themselves. This whole purdah thing has gone too far. Why should we cover up? Look what happened to women in Afghanistan and Iran. Why can't kaneezes show their faces? If we must hear stories about them, let's at least see what they look like."

We fell silent. Outside, the wind increased, causing leaves and branches to rustle. A storm was brewing. I was glad that the children were home. The woman had said nothing bad would happen to those who were not afraid. But I felt a knot in the pit of my belly.

Saira and Nadia sidled into the room, their eyes large like dinner plates. My heart skipped a beat. "You hungry? Please tell Hasina and Noor to start dinner. We're having burgers and French fries today, remember? That's what you wanted, right?"

"We—we're waiting for Arif and Sameer," Nadia said.

Saira approached me. I noticed tears streaked on her cheeks.

My voice rose. "Waiting for them? Where are they?"

"We were playing cards," Nadia said. "And then Sameer—his sweater—he'd left it in the park. On a rock. He didn't want to lose it."

My heart bounced against my chest, pounding blood in my ears. I felt as if I were perched on a tree, listening to Saira's voice. "So where are the boys?"

"Gone—to get the sweater," Saira gulped. "They said they'd run there and back—the sun was still up."

"How long ago was this?" Heera asked the question.

Nadia seemed to deliver her response a day later: "Like... one hour..."

twenty-three

LAILA

Yasmeen slumps on the sofa, her face pale. She opens her mouth, and closes it as if she cannot trust the words that she might release. Fazila reaches out for her cousin's hand, but Yasmeen does not respond. She clutches the sofa arm. I sit transfixed, images of cobra plants knotting my mind, black robes coating my tongue, preventing me from speaking. Heera places her arm around my shoulders.

Shireen turns to Nadia and takes charge. "Tell us again—what happened?"

Nadia gulps. "We were playing cards. The room got cold. Sameer looked for his sweater. He couldn't find it. Right?" She turns to Saira, who huddles beside Yasmeen, for confirmation.

Saira nods, a hiccup jolting her body.

"Then what?" Shireen pushes.

"He didn't want to tell you guys that he'd lost the sweater. The sun was up, and they decided to go get it. They made us promise not to tell you."

Shireen's mouth is a straight line. "Go on."

Nadia looks at her feet. "Saira and I started reading our books. We noticed that darkness had fallen. And that's when we realized that the boys had been gone for some time—"

Shireen shakes her head. "I'm sure they're okay. Like you, they were distracted. We'll find them." She laces her shoes. "Nadia, you're

185

the eldest. You should have known better than to let them break rules."

Nadia's hair falls across her face. She joins Saira, who sat on the sofa, tears trickling down her cheeks. "I didn't know..."

I walk to the door. I have to look for my grandson.

"Wait here," Shireen mutters. "I'm going to get Aslam and the chowkidar."

Heera and I put on our walking shoes while Fazila comforts Yasmeen. "There's no need to panic. They're probably outside playing." But the strain in her voice reveals her own fear.

Yasmeen doesn't respond.

As soon as Shireen returns with the chowkidar Mohammed and the driver Aslam, Heera and I pick up our umbrellas. "We're going with them," I say.

Shireen nods. "I'll stay with the girls. The boys may show up here."

"I want to go." Yasmeen lifts herself off the sofa, but Saira's arms are wrapped around her mother's waist.

I whisper in Yasmeen's ear. "Stay here with your daughter. We will bring Sameer back. If we need your help, we'll send someone for you. Don't leave Saira alone..."

Yasmeen wraps her arms around Saira and kisses her daughter's forehead. The fear in her eyes rolls like loose marbles.

Outside, trees rustle as if a helicopter chops through branches. The gusts tug at my kurta and yank my hair loose. I wrap my chaddar around my ears, bending to shield myself from flying leaves.

Aslam watches Heera and me struggle in the dark. "Memsahib, please go inside. We will find the boys."

I shake my head and follow Aslam and Mohammed, who stride ahead, their torches bobbing as twilight bleeds into the inky night. We reach the end of the road and turn toward the park. Clouds have returned and drizzle—mist sheerer than a spider's web—hangs in the air. We trample forward, pushing past the wetness that clings to our lips, our eyelashes, and the tips of our noses. Our open umbrellas cannot shield us from the horizontal wind.

Even though we walk through mist, we don't have to descend to note that the park is deserted. I discern motionless swings. Around us, in the darkness, long strings of cobra plants hang past leaves' edges like quivering snake tongues. Taking a breath, I remind myself that cobra plants have roots and that the stories that surround the plants are not true. But in the darkness, I cannot remain coherent.

The steel slide glints. I drop my umbrella against a tree and cup my hands around my mouth to call: "Same-e-e-er! A- a-a-rif!"

No response. Aslam and Mohammed descend the stairs to the center of the park to see if the boys are hiding in a place that cannot be seen from above. The streetlights are not working, and we are surrounded by darkness. Clouds block the full moon. Pine trees sway. I shiver and call the boys' names again. This time, we hear a footfall behind us.

"Nani?" Arif emerges from behind a pine tree, rubbing his eyes. His cheeks are streaked with dirt and tears while his jeans are torn at the knee.

I gather him in my arms. "Are you all right? Where is Sameer?"

"He—" Arif gulps. "He's gone."

"Gone? What do you mean?"

Arif gulps, his body shivering.

I wrap my shawl around him, but his teeth continue to chatter. Crying, he rubs dirt-covered fists in his eyes. Heera and I walk him to a bench, and I shine my torch on him. The beam reveals grass stains on his pant knees and scraped elbows.

"What happened?"

He shakes his head. "I slipped. I'm okay."

I stroke his back, waiting for his tears subside. "Arif, you have to tell us—where is your cousin?"

Arif scuffs his shoes. "We reached the park. The sweater was where Sameer left it. He told me to wait while he went down to get it."

"What happened next?"

"I heard him yell to say that he was coming up the stairs. Then, I heard voices and saw two men. They had mustaches and carried walking sticks."

My heart skips a beat.

Arif shakes his head. "I didn't want them to see me, so I hid behind a tree. The mist was thick. I could hear their sticks hitting the road."

"Go on."

"I stayed hiding for a long time. The guys just stood by the stairs of the park. They were talking. I heard bumping sounds. Like they were hammering something. I waited. Then their voices faded."

"What happened next?"

Arif rubs his eyes. "Once I was sure they had gone, I ran down the stairs..."

A clap of thunder collides. "And where was Sameer?"

Arif begins to cry again. "Sameer—he wasn't there. I looked for him everywhere. He was gone. I called him and called him. He didn't answer. Maybe the men took him."

"Did the men talk to him?"

"No. I don't know."

A howl floats from one of the nearby trees. Arif clutches my arm.

"It's an owl," Heera says.

I understand his fear. I feel as if I am slipping down a torrential waterfall into a river swollen with rain. Telling Heera to stay with Arif on the bench, I step across the road and shine my torchlight on the grassy steps leading into the slopes of the park. Another owl hoots. I hear a scampering sound—a squirrel or another rodent.

I descend into darkness mumbling a prayer, my torchlight barely cutting through the fog. I know that I have reached the flat center of the park when the steps end. Using my light, I walk toward the slab where Sameer's sweater had been. My light reveals the dull stone. At least my grandson is warm. I call his name, but get no response, except for a hollow echo. Aslam and Mohammed have already checked inside the park, but I walk along its curve, praying for signs of Sameer's presence. I climb up the stairs again where Arif and Heera await me.

"We need to return to the house," Heera says. "Arif is cold and wet. His mother needs to know he's safe."

"You take him back. I'm going to stay here. Sameer has to be somewhere close." I stand up, folding my arms against my chest. They found Yasir, still breathing. But he died. Overexposure, wrote the doctor in the death certificate. I have to find Sameer. "Aslam is with me. I will stay."

High above, crows caw. I shiver, reminded of stories I have heard and fabricated. Heera and Arif head toward the house.

"I'll be back very soon—with Sameer," I call to their receding backs. "Tell Yasmeen not to worry." I sit on the bench and tap my umbrella on the gravel road, trying to distract myself from the fear I taste in my mouth.

Aslam melts into the mist to get some help from the local police officer, leaving me to continue my tapping, trying to generate a picture in my mind of Sameer safe at home. Someone once told me that visualizing happy moments can transform into real experiences. I focus on Sameer playing cricket, racing up and down the park stairs, his hair quivering with excitement, but I can't set aside the image of Yasir, his ankle broken, lying on the side of the road, trying to crawl home in the rain.

Aslam returns with Hawagali's policeman, Khan Sahib, a thick-mustached man with a squeaky voice that makes him sound as if air is stuck in his throat. With him are ten men from the village; Khan Sahib separates them into four groups, outlining directions for each party to search. He gives each leader a whistle that is to be used when Sameer is found.

I cling to the phrase when Sameer is found, but my mind feels like an open radio channel gathering static, interfering with my efforts to picture Sameer happy and strong. The edge of my shalwar is caked in mud. As I walk by a tree, my kurta catches against a twig and tears. One of the men in my group, a boy not much older than eighteen, stays close to me. My toe hits a sharp stone.

"Madam, go home," the boy says. "We will find your grandson."

I stare into his smooth face. So young. "No."

He nods, breaks off a stick and hands it to me to use as a cane. "Then we shall find him together."

The confidence in the boy's voice gives me energy. I walk beside my companion, noticing that he drops his pace to match mine. A water pellet pierces my skin, followed by another before torrents of rain descend upon us. I discarded my umbrella somewhere, and I am getting soaked. I have to find Sameer. My companion, Sajid, and I reach the wooden shelter in Titlipark. My knees are wobbly. I sit down.

Sajid looks out of the shelter at the green lawns of the park, now a lake. "Madam, your grandson is fine. Allah is with him."

Long ago, I gave up my belief in god, but standing beside Sajid, I feel a resurgence of hope. When the rain clears, soggy and tired, we return to the bench where we started out. Sajid urges me to return to the house. "You must rest, Madam."

I shake my head. A torchlight floats through the darkness. Yasmeen, along with Heera and Fazila, has joined the search. Heera hands me a raincoat. I drop it over my shoulders although my skin is already drenched.

"The policemen will find Sameer," Fazila says. "He'll be fine. I know it." She leaves us on the bench and returns to the house to be with her son and comfort the children.

Yasmeen, Heera, and I walk along the mountain paths, calling for Sameer, with Sajid, our silent supporter, who walks with us. Sometime during the night, Shireen joins us to report: "Fazila's with the children. She's trying to get them to rest. Saira wouldn't stop crying, and Arif's begging to go out and look for his younger cousin. She's having them play imaginary games with Sameer."

Close to two in the morning, Khan Sahib tells the villagers to go home. "Madam, we shall wire to Murree and to the other hill stations. We will find your son. Please rest. We will find Baba."

My mind races from one scenario to the next, wondering if the men were kidnappers, and if Sameer, bound and gagged, is being taken to a beggar camp. From behind thick clouds, the moon pierces through. This is the night the cobra plants are supposed to come alive.

twenty-four

LAILA

"Maybe we should go inside?" Heera touches my arm. "We are tired—your body is soaked. We're not thinking straight. Hot tea and a change of clothes will do us good."

I leave Yasmeen on the bench and go to the house to change into dry clothes. When I return, outside, Yasmeen sits at the same spot, her body unmoved.

I pull her cold hand into mine and massage it. "You'll catch a cold. Come, let's go inside?"

She shakes her head. She is remembering that other night.

"Baita, circumstances are different. Don't remain in the past. Let it go."

But I, too, cannot dismiss Yasir's dimpled cheeks that I saw before his body was carried by his uncles and cousins to the grave. "Sameer is young. The circumstances that led to that... accident are not here tonight. You must believe that." Perhaps if I repeat the words to myself, I can accept them as truth.

"Come on, Baita, walk with me, so we can be warm." I press her hand and draw her down the road. Yasmeen allows me to lead her. We fix our eyes on the markers at the edge of the streets, trying to avoid water that slams into rocks. Without direction, we walk until we reach a fork. The uphill turn leads to Titlipark, while the other, a downhill path is one that I have not walked for almost two decades.

Tariq stays in Hawagali for two weeks. After drinking vodka tonic, he falls asleep in the living room. I drop a blanket over him and thrust a pillow beneath his head. Unable to stop myself, I wrap a chaddar around my body and I slip into the night, walking down this path until I reach the cottage where I have spent many afternoons.

I enter the cottage with a key Athar gave me, loosening my hair. Dropping on the bed beside Athar, I place my mouth close to his and inhale his onion breath. I draw his hands out from the blanket, smiling when he awakens, his eyes alive with surprise.

At four in the morning, before the sun reappears, I walk uphill to my house, letting myself in through the back door. I slip past Tariq still asleep on the sofa, and lie down on my own bed, aware that my teeth are chattering because of the risks that I am willing to take.

*   *   *

Yasmeen and I turn a corner. We stand in front of the one-roomed cottage that I know too well. The white fence is battered, while the windows are boarded.

Yasmeen stops. "This is the house, isn't it?

"Yes."

Yasmeen's face is covered with tears, as is mine.

*   *   *

I sit at my dressing table, combing my hair, wondering how to let Athar know about Yasmeen's sickness. The Toyota screeches in the driveway.

From the window, Tariq's voice floats up, "Where is she? Where is that witch?"

My fingers curl over my comb, wishing I could be whisked away from the bedroom into safety. Tariq's footsteps stomp up the stairs. When he flings the door open, I summon up a smile to greet him.

He leans against the slammed door, his arms crossed. "So, you're going out, I hear. Would you care to tell me where you might be headed?"

From across the room, I can smell the whiskey sweat on him. I stammer, "To see Heera."

"You witch!" Tariq explodes. I am braced for his slap across my face, but the force sends me sprawling on the bed. "You whore! Who is he, this hijra you are fucking? You tell me now!"

I shake my head. "No. No one."

Tariq's face pushes against mine. His mouth reeks of stale whiskey and cigarettes. "Tell me."

My breath stops. I have to calm him and slip away, so I can tell Athar that Tariq might have learned about us, about my plan to leave him. My airline ticket lies on Athar's table with my new name, Mrs. Athar Khan, alongside my fake passport, showing my photograph without any jewelry that Tariq gifted me. I remind myself that my husband could not know about my lover. He has always been suspicious, even when I wasn't seeing Athar. But tonight, he has reason to believe what he does. My heart rattles against my chest.

Tariq breathes into my face. "You tell me!"

I feel faint and blink at black spots that dance in front of my eyes. Pushing past my throbbing cheeks and arms, I focus on the one way I know to distract my husband. I remove my kurta and unhook my bra.

Tariq's breath quickens, his interest shifting. I have never permitted him to see me with so few clothes. Tariq draws me close and presses his head between my breasts, his mustache a razor against my skin and his words, sharp knives: "You witch, seduce me like you seduced your pimp."

"I love only you. My heart beats only for you." I'm lying for my life, for Athar's life, for the children's lives. "Let me show you." His hands remain on my body, squeezing me, but my heart is ready to pop out of my chest and plop on the floor, a tangle of blood and veins.

* * *

I drop my pace. Yasmeen's hand slips away. Conscious of the blister forming at the bottom of my foot, where my heel scrapes against a stone lodged in my shoe, I say: "I did injustice to your father by marrying him. My family pushed me. We were wrong, and he repaid me with rage. But how can I regret an act that brought you into my life? Without him, you wouldn't be here with me today."

"I don't believe that he was our father..."

"There's nothing that I can say that will sway you from your thoughts." The cottage has melted into the mist and our path is uphill. Neither one of us wants to stop walking.

"Yasir's dimples weren't from Abu's side, nor from your side."

I shake my head. "Baita, let it go. That's not to say that I didn't dream of being with... the other. But we reencountered each other after you were a teenager... after he came to Hawagali, long after you and Yasir were born ... only then..."

"Why didn't you leave Abu?" Her voice is flat. When I touch her back, she shivers.

"I couldn't leave your father, Yasmeen. Not after... everything that happened."

And I tell her about how Tariq, enraged to find me gone, went looking for me in his car. In the mist, his car hit an object. When he returned to the house and went back outside on foot, he found Yasir soaked in the rain. His ankle was broken, and he had a gash on his side. Blood soaked through his shirt because of an internal hemorrhage caused by impact with a rock or something else.

"Your father was convinced that he hit Yasir, that he caused your twin's accident," I tell Yasmeen. "But the doctor wrote: 'Death due to overexposure and double-pneumonia.' Your father didn't believe that. 'Take me to the police,' he told me. He pulled his remaining hair by the roots and cried. 'Just take me to the police now. Lock me up,' he pleaded. But I couldn't—how could I? I forgave your father."

Yasmeen's voice is soft. "You're saying that... Abu... Abu caused Yasir's death? That Yasir would have lived if...?" She repeats her words as if she needs to hear them herself.

I shake my head. "The doctor found no evidence that a car had hit him. A falling log could have crushed his rib. Your father spoke out of guilt. Who is to know the truth?"

"And that night... you told Abu... you told him about your...?"

"I didn't need to say anything. Your father knew. 'I should never have married you,' he repeated. 'I should have left you for the other. Take me to the police. Let me go and you will be free.'

"But I couldn't. The only way I could forgive myself was by forgiving your father. And after that night, your father was a different man. He aged and lost his rage. Often, he fell asleep at night with his eyes wet. And you were having nightmares. I couldn't leave... And after you flew away to college, I could not leave the life I knew."

In the silence, toads' croaks are punctuated by whirring crickets and an owl's hoot. Yasmeen walks faster, away from me toward the park. Water from branches splatters on her shoulders.

"It's no use," she calls. "Sameer's gone. Like Yasir, Sameer is gone."

twenty-five

YASMEEN

My legs wobbled as if they were made from melted wax. I stumbled to the edge of the park. Ignoring tears that rolled down my cheeks, I walked faster. Anything could happen on the mountainside: Sameer could trip and fall, cobra plants could wrap around him, a car could hit him, or he could break his ankle and roll down the mountainside. The road ahead of me wound along the hillside like a dragon's tail, fire awaiting me at the tip.

"Be careful, Baita." Amman's voice was a wail, pushing me into the swirling wind.

Stumbling into the mist, I walked down the road. If I drifted far enough, I would dissolve as if I were water.

From far away, as if from another mountaintop, Amman called: "Wait for me!"

"On my own," I whispered. Tears streamed down my cheeks. Sobs like broken glass were caught in my throat, rolling off my tongue, out of my nose. Around me was darkness.

I felt like Gerda in the fairy tale The Snow Queen, Gerda, the girl who lost her friend when ice fell in his eye. Except that I was the one with ice-shards in my eye, and my vision had been distorted for decades. In the story, Gerda's friend cried so much that the ice fell out of his eye, letting him see again. Tears cascaded down my cheeks as I wept. The ice in my eyes slipped away in the river of tears that I had shed for eighteen years.

I stared at stars that flickered through thinning clouds and slowed my pace. That night I was certain that I could read everyone's mind, but I did not know anything. I didn't know that Amman was getting ready to leave with her lover, I didn't know that Abu was drunk. I didn't register Yasir's hazy eyes the last time he kissed my forehead before he went down to talk to Abu.

I stepped into puddles, splashing water on my jeans, oblivious of drops that sprinkled on my body as wind stirred branches.

*   *   *

I sweat in bed, aware of Amman's jasmine perfume.

From downstairs, I hear Abu's voice rumble like hail pelting the roof. "Where are you?"

Yasir's voice is a spurt like water dripping from a garden hose. "Coming." Yasir rattles down the staircase from the attic, his favorite spot in the house where he sits by the window and blows smoke at the tree, the home of the kaneezes. On his way to Abu, Yasir looks into my room, grinning. I know that his smile will be wiped away when he reaches the bottom of the staircase where Abu awaits.

Yasir kisses my forehead. "Feeling better?"

I nod, happy to have him close to me. Abu shouts for him again.

Yasir ruffles my hair. "I better see what he wants." His face is paler than usual, and his unshaved beard is pepper on his chin. His footsteps thump, as his feet tackle stairs two at a time.

More rumble. "Your mother? Where is she?"

Yasir's voice is a trickle. He doesn't know.

Abu's drumbeat is louder. "Your eyes are red! Empty your pockets. My son is a charsee. Show me what you have!"

I struggle to get out of bed but fall against my pillow. My fever has stripped my strength. Abu's deep boom is followed by laughter. Yasir smokes hash often, but never when Abu's around. I've smoked with Yasir. Though I enjoy the sweet taste, I don't appreciate the dizziness.

One night when I walked up to the attic, I saw Yasir sitting on a beanbag by the window. He held foil with one hand, and with the other, he lit a flame beneath black putty, opium. Using a straw, he snorted the smoke. I approached him as he closed his eyes. "You should try it," he said. "The neighbor gave me some. It's free. I'd never buy it..."

Abu's shouts escalate while Yasir's voice sinks lower.

I hear thuds as if a person hits a wet sheet: I recognize the sound of Abu punching the wall. One punch lands somewhere on Yasir's body. Yasir falls, but forces himself to his feet, swearing at Abu under his breath. The front door slam is a gunshot. Yasir leaving the house.

Rain pours outside, and he walks out without a raincoat.

*　　*　　*

My pace accelerated as I stepped through puddles. Pictures of the night cascaded through my mind, falling like snow, melting, and sticking. The glass had fallen out of my eye, and the scene lay before me: Abu drunk, Amman with her lover, while Yasir tried to find escape. Sick in bed, I was too blind to know the truth.

I sat on the white mile marker by the side of the road to stare at clearing clouds. In the distance, early morning rays peaked over the mountaintops.

I heard a voice. Yasir lay by a tree, cobra plants swaying around him. High above kaneezes floated and rotated. I heard Yasir's voice again. The fog lifted as if someone had opened curtains to a stage. When I reached the tree, the first ray of sunlight touched the bark where I had seen Yasir's shoulder.

My heart skipped a beat. A figure half of Yasir's size rubbed his eyes. Sam. Golden rays pierced through the mist and kissed his black hair, which stood up as if every unruly curl waved hello to me.

"Mom!"

I scooped Sam in my arms, lifting him to hug him. His weight pushed me down to the pebbled road. Ignoring stones that dug into my thighs, I kept Sam in my lap, stroking his cheeks and trying to read his eyes, heavy with sleep. His body was dry. He had found shelter while the family and villagers searched for him in the rain.

I examined his face, hands, legs—not a scratch. Sam wore Yasir's old sweater. I mopped my tears with my shawl, thinking of my twin who used to dream the endings of my dreams. He had left us. And my dreams—in Karachi, Hawagali, or Houston—were for me to finish and to start.

Amman and Heera found us sitting in the middle of the road, with me rocking Sam in my lap, the boy too big.

twenty-six

LAILA

Sameer sits on the sofa with his mother beside him. I wrap a blanket around them and drop into the rocking chair. The storm has ended and my grandchildren are home. The rest of the children crowd around the bathed boy, who grins and sips chicken soup.

"Did you see kaneezes?" Nadia asks.

"What happened to you?" Saira asks.

My daughter pulls her son closer. She does not need to say anything.

Sameer glances around the room and clears his throat. "I'll tell you the story. You know that I left the sweater in the park, right? So Arif and I had to go get it. It was dark when we reached the park. I told him to wait on the street, while I ran down the stairs. But when I came up, these guys were standing there. So I waited till they walked away. And I didn't see Arif."

"I was behind a tree!" Arif says.

Sameer makes a face at his cousin. "I didn't see you. So I went inside the house—you know, the one that's across from the park."

"You what?" everyone speaks together.

Sameer looks around the room, holding on to the moment of suspense. He shrugs. "It's not a big deal. The side door of the house wasn't locked. I ran in when the men weren't looking. The inside was dark and no one was around. Most of the house was empty. But I didn't feel scared. In one room, a lamp was lit. And there was just one brown sofa that looked clean, so I lay down and fell asleep."

Again everyone expostulates: "You what?"

Sameer laughs. "What? I was tired. I fell asleep. What's wrong with that?"

We had been combing the countryside, weeping, remembering how we had lost Yasir, and the entire time Sameer was a short distance from us, sleeping. Used to the house being locked-up and empty, we didn't even knock on the front door or walk around the premises.

"When I woke up, there was this lady," Sameer continues. "She had weird eyes, like purple."

"Mom, he's making things up now." Saira tugs her mother's arm.

"Let him continue," Yasmeen says.

Sameer rubs his eyes. "She gave me warm milk. She looked scary with her eyes and red hair, but she was nice. She wore black clothes. I asked her if she was a kaneez and she laughed. She wouldn't tell me if she was one."

"Then what?"

"She said everyone was looking for me. She told me to go outside when the rain stopped. And I remembered, you know, how Nani says not to go out in the rain? I stayed inside, so I didn't get wet." He paused and looked at his mother. "I remembered the rule about not being outside alone—especially at night. The woman was a stranger, but she was nice. She told me to wait till the sun came out."

"What happened next?" Yasmeen holds Sameer close to her heart.

"Nothing. The sun came up and I went outside—the lady was with me. She said she'd stay till we saw Mom. And that's what happened."

"I didn't see her," Yasmeen says.

"She was there. Mom, can we visit her tomorrow?"

"We can try," Yasmeen says.

But the woman with the purple eyes won't be at the house, I comment to myself.

*   *   *

After the children are tucked in, Yasmeen joins me in my room where I sit on my bed, wearing a worn-out nightgown.

Seeing the surprise in her eyes, I say, "I found the nightdress in my old clothes that I left here. Soft cotton." I pause. "And you? You're fine with everything I told you?"

Yasmeen nods.

I pat the bed beside me, and Yasmeen joins me, curling into a ball, her head in my lap. I stroke her hair.

Just when I think Yasmeen's fallen asleep, she sits up. "I better go down," she says. "I left my purse lying downstairs. It's stuffed with important papers. You know ticket, passport, and everything."

I lift my hands off her hair.

She sits up, and shakes her head. "No, forget it. Why do I have this compulsion to lock everything?"

"Your father was that way."

"Abu." She lets out a deep breath. "Yes, I remember how he used to scold us if we didn't lock the car or our doors. I need to shed that habit. You know Yasir was crazy that night, don't you?"

"Yes."

She opens her mouth and then closes it. "You shouldn't feel as if the accident was your fault," she finally says. "It wasn't anyone's fault."

My eyes caress her face. Tears streak her cheeks, but her face is peaceful. "I'm sorry for being so angry with you."

I nod and comb my fingers through her tangled hair. My daughter is talking to me, and I am listening. We have more stories to share and much to learn together.

twenty-seven

YASMEEN

I look around the room where my grandparents used to stay when we visited the mountains. The only one sitting upright on the king-size bed, I have a full audience. This June visit, the largest room in the house—and the space the children covet the most—was won through a lottery by the girls, Nadia and Saira. But tonight, all family members have found spots to plant their bodies. Two decades after the renovation of the Hawagali house, the walnut cupboard is polished and its dark patches are gone. The desk by the window is new and bookshelves are filled with Urdu and English books that my uncle stocked up for the family's grandchildren.

The bed that used to creak has a new mattress, but the oil stain on the wooden headrest is a reminder of many oil-massaged heads that have reclined against the back. The walls and floor are polished, and the room is lit by the fire and by candles planted on side-tables, bookshelves, and the mantelpiece.

I run my fingers through Sam's hair, still damp from his bath. Warmth from the fire will soon dry it out, and his hair will return to its springy texture. Nadia and Arif lie on their stomachs on each side of their aunt while Saira sprawls at the foot of the bed, her eyes pinned on her favorite aunt, Fazila. Sprinkled beyond the bed are Amman, Shireen Khala, Fazila, and Heera. Fazila paints her nails with a pearl polish that she swears is the hottest shade, while Shireen Khala sways on the rocking chair. On the sofa recline Amman and Heera, their feet on the coffee table and their heads turned toward the window that offers a view of the mountains.

I look around the room. "So, a story before bedtime?"

"Yes," echo the children. They are already creating stories in their imagination, and I wonder if my tale will be redundant.

"Ji," adds Sam showing off his Urdu.

I ruffle his hair and begin:

*   *   *

One evening, when I was in Hawagali with the family, the weather was cold and rainy much like today. My brother and I listened to music in the attic. Someone called my name. I asked my twin to turn down the music, but he didn't hear me. I got up and went downstairs.

Heera waited for me at the bottom of the stairs. When she saw me, she placed her finger on her lips. "Do you want to see something?" she asked me.

She opened the front door to welcome a beam of sunshine. Rain and cold had melted. I don't know how to explain what I saw, but nighttime was wiped away, and we stepped into broad daylight. In the front garden, running and skipping between the bushes and the fir trees were children of all ages—big, little, teenagers, boys, girls, with long hair, short hair—playing running-catching, cricket, or lying on the grass enjoying sunshine. There were so many that I couldn't even count them.

I wanted to dash upstairs to get my twin, but I was afraid that if I left the doorway, the children would vanish. Instead, I stepped into the garden. My cousin Fazila was also outside. She introduced me to a new friend, a boy named Muzaffar. I noticed that Fazila and Muzaffar were barefoot. I unlaced my boots, leaving my toes free to wiggle in the grass.

They took my hand and led me to a lake that I'd never seen before. We sat on a rock at the edge of the lake and dropped our feet in the cool water. I remember that we didn't talk much. Instead, we listened to the water, the whistle of the mynahs, and the gurgle of the doves.

The birds flew away when we heard leaves rustle as if someone were pushing branches. Turning around, we saw a shadow behind a walnut tree. After all the stories I'd heard about Hawagali, I should have been afraid, but all I wanted to do was step out of the water and follow the shadow. Fazila and Muzaffar also had their eyes fixed on the branches and on the shadow that appeared and disappeared. We clambered off the rock and ventured into a forest that had sprung up.

The dark shape vanished, and we found ourselves at the foot of a mountain in front of a cave. Holding each other's hands, we ducked our heads and entered the cave. Once our eyes adjusted to the light, we noticed an old woman sitting in a corner.

She had gray hair that fell around her face, and she wore beads around her neck. I remember thinking that she could have been a beggar, but she didn't ask for anything. I noticed her deep wrinkles and her violet eyes. I didn't know that anyone could be so old. Normally, I would have been afraid of a stranger, but she was soothing. We knew. The woman had wisdom.

We sat on the sand with her, and she told us about army tanks, fires, and ashes. We would see them, she said, in our lifetime. She said that there would be destruction, but we would be surrounded by music and song. She reminded us of how poets and artists express truth without fear. "Each of you has a battle to fight," she said. "We will sing for you to help you in your struggle."

As she fell quiet, we heard women singing in a language that I didn't recognize. Their voices were from behind a rippling brook at the back of the cave.

The woman taught us how to spin musical stories so we could find joy. She showed us how to draw figures in the sand and on cave walls. We sang together, told stories to each other, and we drummed on the rocks. When the moment to leave set in, we knew. We stood up and wished her farewell.

As we left the cave, she called out: "Remember, we will always sing for you."

Fazila, Muzaffar, and I left the cave and returned to our garden. By then, the rest of the children had gone away, and the sun was setting. We reentered the house where my mother, Fazila's mother, Heera, and Yasir waited for us at the dinner table.

* * *

Saira sits up. She's always the one to ask questions—Sam is half asleep while Nadia and Arif are thinking of something else. "Did this really happen?"

207

I flip around so I can be at the foot of the bed with Saira. I put my arms around her. "Someone always sings for us. Ask Fazila Khala. She'll tell you if the story is true."

Saira props her chin up with her palms. "Well?" she asks her aunt.

Fazila adds a coat of silver on her thumbnail. She looks up and nods. "Of course the story is real. The woman is still in the cave. She sings for each one of us. Every day."

Acknowledgments

When long-time friend, fellow writer, and Veliz Books co-founder Minerva Laveaga Luna offered to run a second edition of *Black Wings*, I used the opportunity to tighten text and chop 30 pages. The new version of *Black Wings* is a leaner novel that is reflective of the writing style that I developed since the novel's first edition was published by Alhamra Publishing. However, the heart of the novel—the healing power of stories and multigenerational exchanges that cross continents—remains constant.

Deep gratitude to friends and family members who are present and to those who have passed on. I cannot begin to list every family member, friend, and colleague who has influenced my life, writing, and the creation of *Black Wings*. For now, thank you to the many who have crossed my path including:

- organizations and individuals for creating new opportunities: Minerva Laveaga Luna, Kristal Acuña, Laura Cesarco Eglin, and the rest of the Veliz Books team for the new edition of *Black Wings*; Shafiz Naz and Alhamra Publishing for releasing the first edition; Muneeza Shamsie for including an adapted excerpt from *Black Wings* in *And the World Changed: Anthology of Short Stories by Pakistani Women Writers*, (Women Unlimited, New Delhi, India); the late Sabeen Mahmud founder of T2F (Karachi, Pakistan); Constance Jones and Syed Azfer Iqbal with US Embassy (Islamabad, Pakistan); Kamran Ali with University of Texas-Austin (Austin, Texas); Gail Hochman with Brandt & Hochman (New York, New York); Rich Yañez with El Paso Community College (El Paso, Texas); Elizabeth Gregory and Vince Lee with University of Houston, Angela Martinez and Courtney Roberts with Black + Gray Studio, and Houston Arts Alliance, KPFT Pacifica Radio, and Voices Breaking Boundaries (Houston, Texas).

- Sissy Farenthold, Bapsi Sidhwa, and the late Alys Faiz for blazing the trail; Sandra Cisneros for inspiration and for starting Macondo Writers Workshop, a rich network of writers that are too many to name; fellow mothers for hangouts, hiking, and carpool: Claudia Avina, Michele Baranski, Catalina Barrios, Karla Spence-Bluestone, Brittany

Burian, Michelle Calva-Despard, Misbah Dadabhoy, Jennifer Dague, Kishwar Jaffer, Ayesha Kamran, Ruquiya Khan, Nina McDonald, Emily Mencken, Lisa Quon, and Shirleen Thorpe; writers' networks including Womxns Write Inn with liz gonzález, Lucy Rodriguez-Hanley, Parisa Vinzant, Lizbeth Coiman, Alicia Vogl Saenz, Deborah Jensen, Marta Mora, and Tisha Marie Reichle; Pasadena Posse with Gerda Govine, Maria Elena Fernandez, Toni Mosley, and Carla Rachel Sameth; and Jamie Asaye Fitzgerald with Poets & Writers (LA).

- fellow writers, supporters, and documentary artists for solidarity and resistance: Carmen Peña Abrego, Tehmina Mani Ahmed, Terri Arellano, Yolanda Alvarado, Margot Backus, Nemata Blyden, Stephanie Chapman, Oui Chatwara S. Duran, Elizabeth Chiao, Marcela Descalzi, Katy Fenton, Christa Forster, Shannon Garth-Rhodes, Maria González, Eric Hester, Paul Hester, Masume Hidayatullah, Jasmina Kelemen, Rich Levy, Vicente Lozano, Salma Bhojani Mahmud, Carolina Monsivais, Rufi Natarajan, Franci Neely, Krupa Parikh, Shaista Parveen, Emmy Pérez, Hope Sanford, Jacsun Shah, Reggie Scott Smith, Michael Stravato, Jaspal Subhlok, Kathleen Sullivan, Beatriz Terrazas, Marina Tristán, Faroukh Virani, Anita Wadhwa, Zohra Yusuf, Ilona Yusuf, Lauren Zentz, and Gwendolyn Zepeda; Oskar Sonnen for being a pillar and for collaging Minal's drawings to create the cover of *Black Wings*' new edition; and Sorayya Khan, Liliana Valenzuela, and Fan Wu for generous words.

- family elders for rich stories and love: Nana, Nanna, Dadiamman, Baba, Saeeda Gazdar, Mushtaq Gazdar, the late Ruqaiya Hasan, Zawwar Hasan, Rashida Iqbal, Shahida Saad, and the late Mohammad Akhtar—Barey Abba—whom I never met but whose story inspired *Black Wings*; cousins and in-laws for laughter: Jill Anderson, Usha Aqeel, Aun Dohadwallah, Aisha Gazdar, Haris Gazdar, Neil Halliday, Irfan Hasan, Nadeem Hasan, Samina Hasan, Waqar Hasan Rashid Iqbal, Shaye Marshell, Noorulain Masood, the late Hassam Qadir Shah, Azra Rahman, Asif Saad, Nausheen Saad, Samina Saad, Sonia Saldívar-Hull, Felix Hull, and Arshia Usmani; nieces Maha Shahid and Myah Sarwar for being; siblings Beena Sarwar and Salman Sarwar for inspiration; parents Zakia Sarwar and the late Dr. Mohammad Sarwar for wisdom and love; Minal Saldivar for daily brilliance; and René Saldivar without whom my story would be incomplete.

SEHBA SARWAR creates essays, stories, poems, and art that tackle displacement, migration, and women's issues. Her essays and poems have appeared in publications that include *The New York Times Sunday Magazine, Asia: Magazine of Asian Literature, Callaloo,* among others, while her short stories appear in anthologies published by Akashic Books, Feminist Press, and Harper Collins India. Born and raised in Karachi, Pakistan in a home filled with artists and activists, Sarwar is currently based in Los Angeles, California with her husband and daughter, from where she writes and teaches.

To learn more about Sehba Sarwar and her work, please visit her website: sehbasarwar.com